Michael Davies is a lifel[...] has always been deeply co[...] to his roots and family. He is a devoted father to four boys and one girl and now a proud grandfather. His life has been rich in both personal and professional experiences.

For 15 years, he worked in management within the retail industry, where he developed strong leadership skills and a deep understanding of teamwork. After many years in retail, he transitioned to a fulfilling role as an Operating Theatre Support Worker at the Countess of Chester Hospital. Over 12 years, he provided essential support to medical teams across all surgical specialties. Later, he moved to Arrowe Park Hospital to concentrate on Urology, a specialty he found particularly rewarding. In addition to his surgical duties, he would assist in the A&E department during high-pressure situations, bringing adaptability and a thorough understanding of operating procedures crucial to patient care.

However, one night after a busy day in the theatre, his life took a sudden turn. He tripped over debris left by builders and suffered a serious lower spine injury, resulting in the loss of feeling in one of his legs. He was no longer able to work, and losing his job triggered a difficult mental health battle. But with the support of his family and children, he fought to find a way forward.

During this time, he decided to write a book, pouring his emotions and experiences into a character of his own creation, his book, *The Veil of Silence*, which will be released on November 19, 2024, became a lifeline. Writing this story not only gave his purpose, but it also helped him heal.

Michael Davies

THE FRACTURED VEIL

AUSTIN MACAULEY PUBLISHERS
LONDON * CAMBRIDGE * NEW YORK * SHARJAH

Copyright © Michael Davies 2025

The right of Michael Davies to be identified as author of this work has been asserted by the author in accordance with sections 77 and 78 of the Copyright, Designs and Patents Act 1988.

All rights reserved. No part of this publication may be reproduced, stored in a retrieval system, or transmitted in any form or by any means, electronic, mechanical, photocopying, recording, or otherwise, without the prior permission of the publishers.

Any person who commits any unauthorised act in relation to this publication may be liable to criminal prosecution and civil claims for damages.

This is a work of fiction. Names, characters, businesses, places, events, locales, and incidents are either the products of the author's imagination or used in a fictitious manner. Any resemblance to actual persons, living or dead, or actual events is purely coincidental.

A CIP catalogue record for this title is available from the British Library.

ISBN 9781035898237 (Paperback)
ISBN 9781035898244 (ePub e-book)

www.austinmacauley.com

First Published 2025
Austin Macauley Publishers Ltd®
1 Canada Square
Canary Wharf
London
E14 5AA

I extend heartfelt gratitude to their children—Evelyn, Aaron, Harvey, Oliver, and Jacob—for their unwavering support and encouragement throughout the writing process. Their invaluable feedback at various stages of the book's development has been instrumental, and their continued belief in the author's vision has made this journey all the more meaningful.

I also wish to extend heartfelt gratitude to Dave Griffiths and Sarah Griffiths, who have been more than friends—they are family. Through every challenge and triumph, their unwavering support, loyalty, and kindness have been a source of strength. Their presence and encouragement have been invaluable throughout this journey, and I am deeply grateful for their steadfast companionship through thick and thin.

Prologue
Shadows of What Was

Mary sat in the dimly lit living room, her fingers tracing the edges of an old, crumpled photograph. The image had faded over time, but she could still make out the smiling faces of herself and John, her ex-husband, standing in front of the little house they'd bought together over a decade ago. In the background of the photo, a pale, wooden crib sat on the porch—a hopeful promise of the family they never had.

The house looked much the same now, but it had aged poorly, just like Mary. The once cheerful yellow paint was peeling, and the garden John had tended so meticulously had grown wild and unkempt. Mary stared at the crib in the photograph, her thumb brushing over its outline. She remembered how John had insisted on buying it before they were even sure she could get pregnant. "It's about faith," he'd said with a hopeful grin. But faith had turned into a bitter ache as time passed, leaving her empty in ways she never expected.

Mary's eyes moved to the mantle, where two small drawings were carefully displayed in mismatched frames. The crude stick figures were labelled in childish scrawls: *Mummy, Emily* and *Daniel.* She had found the frames at a charity shop years ago, and while they didn't match, they added a sense of pride to the house. She glanced at the drawings every day to remind herself of the life she had built. A life she had fought for.

"I should've thrown it all away," she muttered to herself, her voice breaking the oppressive silence of the house. But her gaze returned to the drawings, lingering there. The corners of her mouth lifted slightly. "No. They need to stay."

She placed the photograph face-down on the coffee table and stood, her joints stiff and reluctant. The air in the room was stale, carrying the faint scent of mildew and dust. She crossed to the kitchen, pausing in the doorway to glance at the clock on the wall. It was almost 7:30 a.m.

"Breakfast time," she said aloud, straightening her posture. Her voice took on a cheery tone, forced but determined. "Emily, Daniel, up! You'll be late for school!"

The only response was the faint creak of the house settling. For a brief moment, the cheerfulness faltered in her voice, but she quickly recovered. "You don't want to keep your teacher waiting, do you?"

She busied herself in the kitchen, pulling out a frying pan and cracking eggs into it. The oil sizzled loudly, filling the small room with the smell of cooking. Mary turned to the small dining table in the corner, where two plates and two glasses of milk sat untouched. She paused, tilting her head.

"Daniel," she called, softening her tone. "Don't forget to take your tablet today. You know how you get if you skip it."

The frying pan hissed as the eggs began to brown, and Mary quickly turned back to flip them over. She hummed to herself a tune she barely remembered from years ago. It was something her mother used to sing, but she couldn't recall the words. As the eggs cooked, she glanced out the kitchen window. The day was overcast, with grey clouds pressing low in the sky. The lawn was wild and uneven, the grass creeping up the sides of the fence.

"Emily!" Mary called, louder this time. She tried to keep the irritation out of her voice. "Don't make me come upstairs!"

The faint sound of her own voice echoing back to her was the only reply. Her grip tightened on the spatula, and for a moment, her hand trembled. She closed her eyes, took a deep breath, and exhaled slowly. "They'll come down," she whispered. "They always do."

She finished plating the eggs, setting them on the table alongside the glasses of milk. As she stepped back to admire the table setting, a wave of sadness washed over her. The table looked… wrong. Too quiet. Too still. She shook her head and brushed her hands on her apron.

"Don't make me eat alone again," she said, the words barely audible.

Later that morning, Mary stood at the kitchen sink, washing the dishes. Her hands moved in automatic motions, scrubbing the plates and rinsing the glasses. She glanced at the two untouched glasses of milk, her lips pressing into a thin line.

"They'll eat lunch," she muttered, turning back to the sink. "They're just picky eaters in the morning."

The sound of the running water filled the room, drowning out the silence for a while. She focused on the rhythm of her tasks, but her mind wandered to the past. She remembered the mornings she used to spend with John, back when everything felt normal. He'd sit at the table with his newspaper, always skimming the sports section first. They'd drink coffee together, share small jokes, and dream about the life they'd build.

The sound of glass clinking against porcelain snapped her out of her thoughts. A small glass had slipped from her hands and shattered in the sink. She cursed under her breath, staring at the shards as water continued to pour over them.

"I should've been enough," she said, her voice low and bitter. "Why wasn't I enough?"

She grabbed a dishtowel and turned off the water, carefully picking out the glass shards and throwing them into the trash. Her hands trembled as she worked, her thoughts spiralling. She pictured John laughing with someone else now, someone younger, prettier. He was probably still reading the sports section, still drinking his coffee, but with a woman who could give him everything she couldn't.

The thought made her stomach twist, and she pressed her hands flat against the counter, gripping the edge tightly. She closed her eyes, inhaling deeply through her nose. "It doesn't matter anymore," she whispered. "I have Emily and Daniel. That's all that matters."

As the day wore on, the silence in the house became unbearable. Mary wandered into the living room, her footsteps echoing faintly on the worn hardwood floor. She glanced at the drawings on the mantle again, the childlike scrawls of her "children's" names glaring back at her.

She sat on the couch, staring at the blank television screen. Her mind raced, the silence broken only by the faint ticking of the clock in the corner. She thought about the mothers she'd seen in the neighbourhood, walking hand in hand with their children. They always seemed so confident, so proud of their perfect little families. She wondered if they ever felt the weight of loneliness, the ache of being left behind.

"They don't deserve it," she muttered to herself. "They *don't know what it's like to lose everything."*

The thought lingered, dark and heavy, as she sat in the dim light. The whispers began again, faint but persistent, like a distant hum just out of reach. Mary pressed her hands over her ears, shaking her head.

"Stop," she said through clenched teeth. "I don't need to hear this."

But the whispers didn't stop. They never did.

That evening, Mary sat at the dining table again, the room lit by the flickering glow of a single candle. The plates were cleared, the glasses emptied. She folded her hands in her lap, her gaze fixed on the empty chairs across from her. The quiet stretched out, oppressive and suffocating.

She reached for the photograph on the coffee table, holding it up to the candlelight. The crib in the background seemed to glow faintly in the flickering light. She traced the outline of it with her finger, her lips curving into a faint smile.

"Tomorrow will be better," she said softly, her voice laced with both hope and desperation. "I'll make sure of it."

She placed the photograph back on the table and extinguished the candle. The house plunged into darkness, silent once more.

Chapter 1
The Perfect Morning

Mary stood in the doorway of the children's bedroom, her hands on her hips, surveying the space with the critical eye of a mother determined to maintain order. The room, though small, was tidy—each item meticulously placed. A single bed with a blue comforter sat on one side of the room, and a twin bed with a pink quilt occupied the other. The beds were made perfectly, their smooth surfaces undisturbed. On the shelves above the beds, books were lined up in height order, and toys were neatly stored in wicker baskets. She exhaled, satisfied. Everything was exactly as it should be.

"Daniel, Emily, time to wake up!" Mary called, her voice warm and maternal but carrying an undertone of urgency. "Breakfast is ready, and I don't want either of you dragging your feet this morning."

The silence that followed was unsurprising, yet Mary frowned as though it were an unusual occurrence. She stepped further into the room, pausing between the two beds. The curtains were drawn tightly shut, allowing only a sliver of light to peek through the edges, casting faint streaks on the floor.

"Daniel," she said, her tone shifting slightly to one of reprimand. "I don't want to have to remind you again. Up. Now."

Her eyes flicked to Emily's bed. "Emily, I mean it. Don't make me come back in here."

Satisfied with her warning, Mary turned and left the room, leaving the door ajar behind her. She moved briskly down the hallway and into the kitchen, her slippers scuffing softly against the floor. The kitchen, like the rest of the house, was spotless. Mary took pride in keeping her home in order; it was one of the few things she felt she could control.

Breakfast was already waiting on the table: two plates of scrambled eggs with toast and two glasses of milk. She'd prepared her own plate earlier, but it remained untouched at the end of the table. She preferred to wait until the children were seated before eating—she believed it set a good example for them. She glanced at the plates and frowned slightly. The eggs on Daniel's plate were cooling quickly, and Emily's toast was getting soggy where it rested against the eggs. They'd better hurry, she thought.

"Daniel, Emily!" she called again, her voice sharper this time. She leaned against the counter, tapping her fingers impatiently against the edge. She hated when they dawdled. It wasn't like they had much to do today—just a few worksheets and maybe a craft project—but she insisted on keeping them in a routine.

After another moment of silence, Mary sighed and straightened. She walked to the foot of the stairs and cupped her hands around her mouth. "If I come up there and you're not out of bed, there's going to be trouble!" she shouted.

Still no response.

Her jaw tightened, and she returned to the kitchen, muttering under her breath. "They're going to be the death of me," she said, but her lips quirked into a small smile. No matter how much they tried her patience, she loved them more than anything.

She sat at the table, staring at the two empty chairs across from her. The mismatched plates, one chipped and one slightly warped from years of use, were placed precisely where the children always sat. Daniel's chair, the taller of the two, had a booster cushion tied to it even though he was "too old" for it now. Emily's chair, painted pink, was decorated with stickers of unicorns and rainbows.

"Daniel," she said again, her voice softer now, almost pleading. "Emily. Please don't make me eat alone."

The house remained silent except for the faint creak of the walls settling. Mary's smile faltered for just a moment before she reached for her fork. She began eating her eggs, her movements slow and deliberate. She chewed methodically, her gaze fixed on the two plates in front of her. After a few bites, she pushed her own plate aside, no longer hungry.

"I'm not going to save your breakfast this time," she said firmly, addressing the empty chairs. "If you don't eat now, that's it. No snacks later."

After breakfast, Mary began her daily cleaning routine. She started in the living room, picking up invisible crumbs from the carpet with her handheld vacuum. She paused occasionally to straighten the picture frames on the mantle or adjust the position of the throw pillows on the couch. As she worked, she hummed softly to herself a tune from her childhood that she couldn't quite place.

Her gaze drifted to the mantle, where the children's drawings were prominently displayed. She smiled, a warmth spreading through her chest. The pictures were simple but heartfelt—stick figures holding hands, smiling suns, and houses with chimneys that puffed little clouds of smoke. She reached out and straightened one of the frames, her fingers lingering on the glass.

"Daniel, come downstairs and get started on your math," she called over her shoulder. "Emily, I want you to finish colouring that picture you started yesterday. No more excuses."

She waited for a response, her smile tightening as the silence stretched. The whispers began again, faint but persistent, just at the edge of her hearing. They were indistinct, like a conversation taking place in another room. Mary's hand dropped from the frame, her jaw clenching.

"Don't start with me today," she said aloud, her voice sharp. She moved to the window and pulled the curtains aside, peering out at the street. The neighbourhood was quiet, the only movement coming from a tree whose branches swayed in the breeze. She watched for a moment before letting the curtain fall back into place.

Mary returned to her cleaning, her movements more forceful now. She scrubbed at a spot on the coffee table that didn't exist, her lips pressed into a thin line. "I said, don't start with me," she muttered. The whispers grew louder, teasing and mocking her. She dropped the rag she was holding and pressed her hands over her ears.

"Stop!" she shouted, her voice cracking. The sound echoed in the empty house, bouncing off the walls. The whispers stopped abruptly, leaving behind a heavy silence.

Mary stood still, her chest rising and falling as she caught her breath. She lowered her hands slowly, her eyes darting around the room. Everything was as it should be—the furniture in its place, the pictures perfectly aligned, the carpet free of crumbs. But something felt... wrong. She shook her head, dismissing the thought. There was no time to dwell on such nonsense. She had work to do.

As the afternoon wore on, Mary found herself in the children's room once again. She dusted the shelves, rearranged the books, and fluffed the pillows on their beds. She paused at the foot of Daniel's bed, staring down at the comforter. A small wrinkle marred its otherwise smooth surface. She bent down to fix it, smoothing her hands over the fabric until it was perfect.

"Daniel, don't forget to make your bed properly next time," she said, her tone gentle but firm. "You're old enough to take responsibility for your things."

She moved to Emily's bed, adjusting the quilt and tucking it in neatly at the corners. "Emily, I want you to keep your desk clean from now on. No more leaving your crayons everywhere."

Satisfied, Mary stepped back and surveyed the room. It was perfect again, just as it should be. She smiled, a sense of pride swelling in her chest. "That's better," she said softly.

That evening, Mary sat at the dining table once more, her hands folded neatly in her lap. The children's plates were gone, cleared away after sitting untouched all day. She stared at the empty table, her thoughts drifting.

"I love you both so much," she whispered, her voice trembling slightly. "Everything I do... it's for you."

The house was silent, but Mary didn't seem to notice. She smiled faintly, her eyes shining with unshed tears. "Tomorrow will be better," she said, echoing the words she'd spoken the night before. "I promise."

The room darkened as the last rays of sunlight disappeared behind the horizon. Mary remained at the table, staring into the empty space where her children should have been.

Chapter 2
Whispers in the Silence

The day stretched long and quiet, as it always did. Mary finished tidying the children's room for the second time that day, smoothing the wrinkles in their bedsheets and lining up their shoes by the door. She took a step back, inspecting her work, then gave a satisfied nod. It was perfect—exactly how it should be. She adjusted Emily's stuffed bear, propping it against the pillow, its button eyes staring lifelessly toward the ceiling.

"There," she said softly, her voice warm and soothing. "Now everything's ready for when you come back in here later."

She left the room, pulling the door halfway shut. The children never liked it completely closed.

The hallway was still and dim, with the afternoon light struggling to seep through the curtains she kept drawn tight. Mary paused for a moment, tilting her head as she listened. The house was silent, save for the faint creak of the floorboards beneath her slippers. She frowned. Something felt off, though she couldn't put her finger on it.

"It's too quiet," she muttered.

Her footsteps echoed faintly as she made her way downstairs, her grip tightening on the railing. The house seemed to press in around her, heavy with stillness. Mary hated this part of the day—the hours between morning chores and evening routines. The time when the children were "busy" with their schoolwork upstairs, and she was left alone to keep herself occupied.

She entered the kitchen and busied herself at the sink, scrubbing the breakfast plates with more force than necessary. The sound of running water filled the room, drowning out the oppressive silence.

As she rinsed the plates and stacked them neatly in the dish rack, Mary's thoughts drifted. Her gaze flickered to the window above the sink, where a sliver of the outside world was visible through the curtain. She could just make out the edge of her overgrown garden and the rusting swing set John had put up years ago.

It had been such a thoughtful gesture at the time. He'd spent hours assembling it, sweating under the summer sun, muttering curses as he fumbled with bolts and instructions. Mary had watched from the window, laughing softly to herself, feeling a rare flicker of hope for their future.

Now the swing set was a relic of a life she barely remembered. The chains hung slack, the seats cracked and faded. It hadn't been touched in years.

"Emily's too old for it now anyway," Mary said aloud, breaking her train of thought.

The sound of her voice startled her, bouncing off the walls of the empty kitchen. She shook her head and turned away from the window, grabbing a dishtowel to dry her hands.

As she worked, she began to notice it again—the faint, almost imperceptible hum that seemed to emanate from the walls. She froze, her grip on the towel tightening.

It started softly, barely audible, like a distant whisper carried on the wind. Mary's breath caught in her throat as she strained to listen, her eyes darting around the room.

"Not again," she murmured, her voice trembling.

The whispers grew louder, overlapping and indistinct, like a crowd of voices speaking just beyond the edge of her comprehension. They weren't clear enough to make out words, but their tone was unmistakable—mocking, cruel, accusatory.

Mary dropped the towel and pressed her hands over her ears. "Stop it," she said through clenched teeth. "I don't want to hear this."

The voices persisted, growing sharper, more insistent. Her heart pounded in her chest as she backed away from the sink, her gaze darting toward the ceiling.

"They're not real," she said, her voice shaking. "They're not real."

But the whispers refused to relent, filling her ears with their relentless taunting. She stumbled into the living room, her hands still pressed tightly against her ears. Her knees buckled, and she sank onto the couch, squeezing her eyes shut.

"Leave me alone!" she shouted, her voice cracking.

The house fell silent.

Mary sat frozen, her chest heaving as she waited for the voices to return. The quiet was deafening, pressing down on her like a physical weight. Slowly, she lowered her hands from her ears, her fingers trembling.

"It's just my imagination," she whispered. "It's nothing. Nothing at all."

She forced herself to stand, her legs shaky beneath her. She couldn't let herself spiral. Not today. The children needed her to keep it together.

The rest of the afternoon passed in a blur. Mary threw herself into her tasks, scrubbing the kitchen counters, vacuuming the living room rug, and rearranging the knick-knacks on the mantle. She kept the television off; the sound of the news only made her anxiety worse. Instead, she hummed softly under her breath, filling the silence with her own voice.

By the time she finished cleaning, the sun had begun to dip below the horizon, casting long shadows across the room. Mary glanced at the clock on the wall—it was nearly time to start dinner.

She climbed the stairs to check on the children, her footsteps slow and deliberate. The hallway was bathed in a faint orange glow from the setting sun, the light spilling through the small window at the end. She paused outside the children's room, her hand hovering over the doorknob.

"Emily? Daniel?" she called softly.

There was no response.

She hesitated for a moment before pushing the door open. The room was just as she'd left it—tidy, quiet, and perfectly still. Her gaze swept over the beds, the shelves, and the little desk in the corner where Emily liked to draw. Everything was in its place.

Mary stepped inside, her heart sinking as she looked around. The room felt empty in a way she couldn't quite describe. She moved to Daniel's bed and sat down on the edge, smoothing her hands over the comforter.

"I don't know what I'd do without you two," she said softly.

Her voice broke the stillness, but it did little to dispel the feeling of unease that had settled over her. She reached out and picked up one of Daniel's toys—a small, plastic dinosaur—and turned it over in her hands.

"You'll always stay with me, won't you?" she whispered.

The faint creak of the floorboards behind her made her freeze. Her breath hitched as she turned, her eyes scanning the room. It was empty.

Mary's pulse quickened as she stood, clutching the toy tightly in her hand. The whispers were back, faint and elusive, weaving through the air like smoke.

"Mummy..."

The single word sent a chill down her spine. It was soft, almost inaudible, but it was enough to make her blood run cold.

"Who's there?" she demanded, her voice trembling.

The room was silent.

Mary's hand shot out, flicking on the light switch. The sudden brightness flooded the room, casting the shadows into sharp relief. She turned in a slow circle, her eyes darting to every corner, every crevice. There was nothing there.

"Get out," she hissed, her voice low and venomous. "This is my house. My family. You don't belong here."

The silence was deafening, but Mary refused to let herself be shaken. She took a deep breath, her grip on the toy tightening.

"I won't let anyone hurt my children," she said firmly.

She turned off the light and left the room, closing the door behind her. The whispers followed her as she descended the stairs, faint but persistent.

By the time she reached the kitchen, they had faded again, leaving her in uneasy quiet. Mary busied herself with dinner, chopping vegetables with precise, almost mechanical movements. Her jaw was clenched, her thoughts racing.

They were trying to get to her. The neighbours, the voices, the shadows—whatever they were. They wanted to take her children away, to leave her alone and broken. But she wouldn't let that happen.

She'd protect Emily and Daniel, no matter what it took.

Chapter 3
A Mother's Devotion

The morning sunlight filtered weakly through the curtains as Mary sat at the kitchen table, her hands wrapped tightly around a steaming mug of tea. The house was quiet, save for the faint hum of the refrigerator and the occasional creak of the floorboards. She stared at the mug, her mind replaying the events of the previous day. The whispers had unsettled her, but she refused to let them take control. She had responsibilities. The children needed her.

Her gaze drifted to the clock on the wall—it was nearly 9:00 a.m. "Emily, Daniel, come down for breakfast!" she called, her voice firm but cheerful.

As expected, there was no response. She took another sip of tea, the warmth spreading through her chest, and set the mug down with a clink. Mary stood and walked to the base of the stairs, cupping her hands around her mouth. "You don't want to be late for your lessons, do you?"

Still nothing. She inhaled deeply, forcing herself to stay calm. The children could be so stubborn sometimes. "Fine," she muttered, brushing her hands down the front of her skirt. "I'll come to you."

Mary climbed the stairs; her footsteps deliberate and steady. She paused outside their bedroom, her hand resting on the doorknob. A faint smile touched her lips. "You'd better be awake," she said lightly.

She pushed the door open, revealing the tidy room she had spent hours perfecting. The beds were neatly made, the books on the shelves precisely aligned, and the toys were organised into their respective bins. She stepped inside, her eyes sweeping the room.

"Emily, you didn't leave your crayons out again, did you?" she said, her tone playful. "You know how much I hate cleaning up after you."

Mary moved to the little desk in the corner, running her fingers over its surface. She picked up a piece of paper, her smile widening as she saw the drawing Emily had "made" the day before. It was a crude but colourful depiction of their family—Mary in the centre, holding hands with Emily and Daniel, with a bright yellow sun in the corner of the page.

She held the drawing close to her chest, her heart swelling with pride. "You're such a talented artist," she murmured. "Maybe we'll hang this one on the fridge."

Mary turned to Daniel's bed, smoothing the already flawless comforter. "Daniel, your math workbook is still downstairs," she said, shaking her head. "You'll need to finish it before lunch."

The silence pressed in around her, but she refused to acknowledge it. She moved to the window and pulled the curtains open slightly, letting a sliver of light into the room. Dust motes danced in the air, catching the sunlight as they swirled lazily.

"You can't stay cooped up in here all day," she said, her voice gentle. "Come on, breakfast is waiting."

Satisfied, Mary left the room, leaving the door ajar. She made her way back downstairs, her mind already racing with plans for the day. The children had worksheets to complete, and she thought they might enjoy making paper crafts later. She'd found a tutorial online for origami animals, and she couldn't wait to show them how to fold a crane.

In the kitchen, Mary set two plates on the table, each one meticulously arranged. Daniel's plate had scrambled eggs and toast cut into neat triangles, while Emily's plate held a smaller portion with a dollop of strawberry jam on the side. She poured two glasses of milk and placed them beside the plates, stepping back to admire her work.

"Breakfast is ready!" she called again, this time with more cheer.

She sat at the table, folding her hands neatly in her lap. The seconds ticked by, the silence in the house growing heavier with each passing moment. She glanced toward the doorway, half-expecting to see Emily and Daniel bounding into the room with eager smiles.

When they didn't appear, Mary's smile faltered. She leaned forward, resting her elbows on the table. "If you don't come down now, your food's going to get cold," she said, her tone edging toward frustration.

She waited a few more minutes before sighing and standing. "Fine. Suit yourselves," she muttered, gathering the plates. She placed them in the oven to keep warm, shaking her head as she worked.

"They'll eat when they're hungry," she told herself, her voice firm.

The rest of the morning passed in a blur of activity. Mary busied herself with housework, scrubbing the kitchen counters until they gleamed and vacuuming the living room carpet for the second time that week. She found comfort in the rhythm of cleaning—it gave her a sense of control, a way to keep the chaos at bay.

She glanced at the clock again—it was almost noon. Mary decided it was time to check on the children's progress with their lessons. She climbed the stairs and poked her head into their room.

"How's it going in here?" she asked brightly.

The room was as quiet and still as ever. Mary stepped inside, her gaze scanning the desks. She frowned when she noticed the math workbook still closed on Daniel's desk.

"Daniel, you haven't even started," she said, her tone stern. She moved to his desk, picking up the workbook and flipping through its pages. "I told you this needs to be done before lunch."

She set the workbook down with a sharp tap, her frustration bubbling beneath the surface. "I don't know what's gotten into you lately," she muttered. "You've been so lazy."

Turning to Emily's desk, Mary picked up a blank sheet of paper and a set of crayons. "Emily, I want you to draw something for me," she said, her voice softening. "Anything you like. Just… try your best, okay?"

She stood in the centre of the room for a moment, her hands resting on her hips. The silence was deafening, but Mary refused to let it bother her.

"I'll be downstairs if you need me," she said finally, her voice trembling slightly. She left the room, closing the door behind her.

Back in the kitchen, Mary prepared lunch—peanut butter sandwiches cut into neat halves, an apple sliced into wedges, and a handful of crackers for each plate. She arranged the food with care, making sure everything looked perfect.

She sat at the table, waiting for the children to join her. The minutes ticked by, each one stretching longer than the last. The stillness of the house seemed to press down on her, heavy and suffocating.

Mary clenched her fists, her nails digging into her palms. "I said it's time for lunch," she called, her voice tight with anger.

When the children didn't respond, something inside her snapped. She stood abruptly, her chair scraping loudly against the floor. "I work so hard for you," she shouted, her voice echoing through the empty house. "And this is how you treat me? Ignoring me like I don't even exist?"

Her breathing was ragged, her chest rising and falling as she glared at the empty chairs across from her. Slowly, the anger drained from her, leaving her feeling hollow. She sank back into her chair, burying her face in her hands.

"I'm sorry," she whispered, her voice trembling. "I didn't mean to yell."

The silence stretched on, unbroken and unforgiving. Mary lifted her head, her eyes red and glistening.

"I love you," she said softly, her voice filled with desperation. "I just want what's best for you."

The afternoon passed slowly, the hours dragging by as Mary moved through the motions of her day. She kept herself busy with little tasks—folding laundry, dusting the shelves, organising the pantry—but her mind was elsewhere.

She couldn't shake the feeling that something was wrong, though she couldn't put her finger on what it was. The whispers had been silent all day, but their absence was almost more unsettling than their presence.

As the sun dipped below the horizon, casting the house in shadow, Mary stood at the window, staring out at the darkening street. The faint glow of a neighbour's porch light flickered in the distance, a lonely beacon in the night.

Mary turned away from the window, her heart heavy. She would do anything to protect her children—anything to keep them safe.

Even if it meant doing things she wasn't proud of.

Chapter 4
The Source of Jealousy

Mary sat on the edge of the couch, her knees pressed together, and her hands gripping the remote control like a lifeline. The faint hum of the television filled the living room, the low volume barely cutting through the silence of the house. She wasn't really watching—just staring blankly at the screen as colourful images flickered in rapid succession.

It was the middle of the afternoon, and her energy was already draining. The stillness in the house felt heavier than usual, pressing down on her like a weight she couldn't shake. She glanced toward the staircase, half-expecting to see Emily or Daniel poking their heads around the corner, but the hallway remained empty.

She flipped through the channels aimlessly, landing on a daytime news segment. A bright-faced anchor-woman beamed at the camera, her blonde hair perfectly styled and her makeup flawless. Mary frowned at the sight of her.

"Of course, you're smiling," Mary muttered. "What do you even have to worry about?"

The woman's voice was cheerful and saccharine as she introduced the next segment. The camera shifted to a reporter standing in a local park, her microphone raised as she spoke animatedly to the audience. Behind her, a small crowd had gathered, their faces glowing with excitement.

Mary leaned forward, her grip on the remote tightening. The words on the screen caught her attention: **"Local Mother's Charity Event Brings Community Together."**

The camera panned to a woman in the centre of the crowd, holding a toddler on her hip. She was radiant, her brown hair pulled into a loose bun and her eyes sparkling with warmth. The toddler giggled and reached for her face, and the woman laughed, nuzzling the child affectionately.

A caption appeared at the bottom of the screen: **"Jemma Theaker—Event Organizer."**

Mary's stomach twisted as she watched the scene unfold. Jemma began speaking into the microphone, her voice light and confident as she thanked the community for their support. Her words were kind and gracious, but Mary barely heard them. Her attention was fixed on Jemma's face—the effortless beauty, the glow of happiness that seemed to radiate from her.

"Must be nice," Mary muttered, her lips curling into a sneer. She turned up the volume, her focus sharpening.

Jemma's smile widened as she talked about the inspiration behind the event. She mentioned her child, her husband, and the joy they brought to her life. The toddler in her arms wriggled and laughed again, drawing a chorus of "awws" from the crowd.

Mary's chest tightened. She turned the volume back down, unable to listen any longer. The sight of Jemma's perfect life—the adoration of the crowd, the love of her family—was like a knife twisting in her gut.

She switched off the television and tossed the remote onto the couch, standing abruptly. Her pulse was pounding in her ears, her breath coming in short, shallow bursts.

"It's all fake," she said aloud, her voice shaking. "Nobody's life is that perfect. Nobody's that happy."

Her words hung in the air, unanswered. She paced the living room, her hands clenched into fists at her sides.

"What does she have that I don't?" she demanded, though there was no one to hear her. "Why does she get to have everything while I have nothing?"

The room offered no response, only the faint creak of the floorboards beneath her feet.

Mary stopped pacing and turned to the window, pulling back the curtain just enough to peek outside. The street was quiet, the neighbouring houses standing in neat, orderly rows. Her eyes darted to the driveway across the street, where a mother was loading groceries into her car while her children played on the lawn.

The sight made Mary's blood boil. She let the curtain fall back into place, her jaw tightening.

"They don't know what it's like," she muttered. "None of them do. They haven't lost everything. They don't know how lucky they are."

Her chest heaved as anger bubbled up inside her, a storm she could no longer contain. She marched to the kitchen, yanking open the drawer where she kept her notepad and pen. She slammed the notepad onto the counter and began scribbling furiously.

The list grew quickly:

1. Jemma Theaker—too perfect. Charity event.
2. Woman across the street—smug. Always smiling.
3. Park mothers—judging me, always whispering.

She underlined Jemma's name twice, her pen pressing so hard it nearly tore through the paper.

"Jemma," she said aloud, testing the name on her tongue. It sounded sickly sweet, like syrup that had turned bitter.

The image of Jemma's face burnt in her mind—the way she laughed, the way she held her child, the way everyone around her seemed drawn to her. It wasn't fair. It wasn't right.

Mary's grip on the pen tightened, her knuckles turning white. She stared at the list, her breathing shallow and uneven.

"They need to understand," she whispered. "They need to see what it's like to lose everything."

The rest of the day passed in a haze. Mary moved through the motions of her routine, cleaning the house and preparing dinner, but her thoughts were consumed by Jemma. The image of her face played on a loop in Mary's mind, a constant reminder of everything she'd lost.

She sat at the dining table that evening, staring at the two untouched plates of food she had prepared for Emily and Daniel. Her own plate sat empty in front of her, the fork untouched.

"Come on, kids," she said softly. "Dinner's ready."

The silence that followed was deafening.

Mary folded her hands in her lap, her fingers twisting together nervously. She glanced at the empty chairs across from her, her heart aching.

"Don't you want to eat with me?" she asked, her voice trembling.

The house remained silent.

Mary's gaze dropped to her hands, her vision blurring as tears filled her eyes.

"You're all I have," she whispered. "Don't leave me."

That night, Mary sat alone in the dark living room, the television off and the curtains drawn tightly shut. The whispers began again, faint and indistinct, like a breeze rustling through leaves.

She pressed her hands over her ears, but it didn't help. The whispers grew louder, more insistent, until they filled her head completely.

"She thinks she's better than you," the voices hissed. "Look at her, flaunting her perfect life. She doesn't deserve it."

Mary squeezed her eyes shut, shaking her head violently. "Stop it," she muttered. "Leave me alone."

The whispers persisted, wrapping around her like a vice.

"She has everything you wanted," they taunted. "Everything you'll never have."

"Shut up!" Mary screamed, her voice cracking.

The house fell silent.

Mary sat frozen, her chest heaving as she struggled to catch her breath. Her hands trembled as she lowered them from her ears, her heart pounding in her chest.

"She doesn't deserve it," she said aloud, her voice barely above a whisper.

The words hung in the air, heavy and final.

That night, as she lay in bed, Mary stared at the ceiling, her mind racing. The whispers had stopped, but their message lingered, seeping into her thoughts like poison.

Jemma's face floated in her mind, taunting her, mocking her. The anger inside Mary burnt hotter, consuming her completely.

"She doesn't deserve it," Mary repeated, her voice firm. "Not anymore."

Her hands clenched into fists at her sides, her nails digging into her palms.

"She's going to understand," Mary whispered. "They're all going to understand."

She closed her eyes, her lips curling into a faint, bitter smile. For the first time in a long time, Mary felt a sense of purpose.

Chapter 5
Watching from Afar

The night was heavy with silence, the kind that wrapped itself around Mary like a suffocating shroud. She sat at the kitchen table, the dim light from the overhead bulb casting long shadows across the room. The list she had started earlier lay before her, the ink bold and angry on the page. Jemma's name stood out at the top, underlined twice for emphasis.

Mary stared at the name, her lips pressing into a thin line. She couldn't stop thinking about the segment on the news—the effortless way Jemma had charmed the crowd, the adoration in her child's eyes, the genuine love in her voice when she spoke of her family. It wasn't fair.

"I'll bet she's never had to struggle," Mary muttered, her fingers tracing over the letters of Jemma's name. "Never had to know what it's like to be alone. To lose everything."

She tore the page from the notepad, folding it neatly and tucking it into her pocket. The act felt deliberate, almost ceremonial, as though she were making a silent vow. She stood abruptly, her chair scraping against the floor, and grabbed her coat from the back of the chair.

The children were already asleep, she told herself as she slipped on her shoes. They wouldn't even notice she was gone.

The streets were quiet as Mary drove slowly through the neighbourhood, her headlights cutting through the darkness. She had no real plan, only a vague sense of purpose that pulled her forward. Her hands gripped the steering wheel tightly, her knuckles white against the black leather.

She passed the park, its empty swings swaying gently in the breeze, and turned down a side street. The houses here were larger, newer, with neatly manicured lawns and spotless driveways. Mary's lip curled in disdain as she scanned the rows of perfect homes, her jealousy simmering just beneath the surface.

Finally, she saw it—the house from the news segment. Jemma's house.

It was even more picturesque in person, a two-story brick home with white shutters and a wraparound porch. Warm light spilt from the windows, casting a welcoming glow onto the neatly trimmed lawn. Mary parked her car a few houses down, turning off the engine and sinking low in her seat.

She watched the house intently, her eyes darting from one window to the next. The living room curtains were drawn, but the soft flicker of a television screen was visible through the fabric. She could just make out the silhouettes of two people sitting close together—Jemma and her husband, no doubt.

Mary's stomach twisted at the sight of them. She imagined them laughing together, sharing stories about their day, basking in the warmth of their perfect life. Her hands clenched into fists, her nails digging into her palms.

"They don't deserve it," she whispered. "They don't appreciate what they have."

Her gaze shifted to the upstairs window, where the light in what she assumed was the child's room was still on. She pictured Jemma tucking her toddler into bed, kissing his forehead, and whispering sweet nothings as he drifted off to sleep. The thought made Mary's chest ache with a hollow, gnawing pain.

For nearly an hour, Mary sat there, watching the house. She noted every detail—the way the porch light flickered slightly, the way the curtains in the living room were pulled just a fraction too far to the left, the way the shadows moved behind the windows. She memorised it all, as though committing the scene to memory would somehow give her control over it.

When the upstairs light finally went out, Mary exhaled slowly, her breath fogging up the window. She waited a few more minutes, just to be sure, before starting the car and driving away.

Back at home, the house was just as she had left it—silent, still, and suffocating. Mary hung up her coat and slipped off her shoes, her movements slow and deliberate. She climbed the stairs to the children's room, pausing in the doorway to peer inside.

The room was dark, the faint glow of the nightlight casting soft shadows on the walls. Mary smiled faintly as she stepped inside, her gaze falling on the two neatly made beds.

"Emily, Daniel," she whispered, her voice barely audible. "Mummy's home."

She sat on the edge of Daniel's bed, smoothing the comforter with her hands. "I missed you," she said softly. "I hate being away from you."

Her eyes flickered to Emily's bed, where the stuffed bear sat propped against the pillow. She reached out and picked it up, cradling it in her arms.

"You're so good," she murmured, her voice trembling. "You don't deserve to be hurt. I won't let anyone take you away from me."

The room was silent, but Mary didn't seem to notice. She pressed the bear to her chest, her tears soaking into its worn fabric.

"They'll understand," she whispered. "I'll make them understand."

The next day, Mary's obsession with Jemma deepened. She found herself thinking about the house constantly, replaying the details in her mind like a film on loop. The flickering porch light. The warm glow from the windows. The shadows moving behind the curtains.

She spent hours at the kitchen table, scribbling notes in her notepad. The list of names grew longer, each one accompanied by a description of why they didn't deserve the happiness they had. Jemma's name remained at the top, circled and underlined, a constant reminder of what Mary had lost.

"She's the worst," Mary muttered as she wrote. "She doesn't even know how lucky she is."

The children's voices echoed in her mind, faint and indistinct, but comforting in their familiarity.

"Mummy, why do you care about her?" Daniel asked, his voice soft and curious.

Mary froze, her pen hovering above the page. She glanced toward the doorway, half-expecting to see him standing there, but the hallway was empty.

"She thinks she's better than us," Mary said aloud, her voice firm. "She doesn't deserve what she has."

Emily's voice chimed in, soft and sweet. "You're better than her, Mummy."

Mary's chest swelled with pride, a faint smile tugging at her lips. "You're right," she said. "We're better than her. We're a family. And we don't need anyone else."

That evening, Mary returned to Jemma's house. She parked a little closer this time, her car hidden partially by the overgrown bushes lining the sidewalk. The house looked just as it had the night before—warm, inviting, and infuriatingly perfect.

She watched as Jemma stepped onto the porch, her child in her arms. They were leaving for an evening walk, Mary realised, her stomach twisting with a mix of jealousy and rage. Jemma's husband joined them a moment later, wrapping his arm around her shoulders as they walked down the driveway.

Mary's hands trembled as she gripped the steering wheel, her nails digging into the leather.

"They don't deserve this," she whispered, her voice shaking. "They don't deserve any of it."

She waited until they were out of sight before stepping out of the car. Her heart pounded in her chest as she approached the house, her footsteps soft and deliberate. She paused at the edge of the porch, her eyes scanning the windows for any sign of movement.

The living room curtains were still drawn, but Mary's gaze lingered on the slight gap where they didn't quite meet.

She could just make out the edge of a picture frame hanging on the wall—a family portrait, no doubt.

Her fists clenched at her sides as she stared at the house, her mind racing.

"This isn't over," she whispered. "Not yet."

Chapter 6
A Memory of Pain

The rain tapped against the windows like a thousand tiny fingertips, the sound rhythmic and soothing to most. But for Mary, the noise was sharp and insistent, clawing at the edges of her mind. She sat in her armchair, staring at the streaks of water racing down the glass. Her thoughts drifted, slipping through her fingers like sand, until they settled on a place she didn't want to go—a place she'd buried deep but could never truly escape.

It was Daniel's face she saw first, not the warm, smiling man she had married, but the version of him from the end. Cold, distant, and hollow-eyed, as if she'd already lost him before he walked out the door.

Her grip on the armrests tightened. "You promised," she whispered, her voice trembling. The house was silent around her, save for the rain and her breathing. "You said you'd never leave."

But promises were only words, she reminded herself. Words that could be broken just as easily as they were spoken.

The memory of the fight came back unbidden, vivid and sharp. They had been sitting at the kitchen table, much like the countless other mornings they'd spent together. Except this time, the air between them was charged, the tension thick enough to choke on.

John had his coffee mug in one hand, his other hand resting on the table. He stared at her with an expression she couldn't quite place—was it pity? Frustration? Maybe it was both. Mary hated it. Whatever it was, it wasn't love.

"This isn't working, Mary," he had said, his voice soft but firm. "We've been trying for years, and... maybe it's time to accept that this might not happen for us."

The words had hit her like a punch to the gut. She had gripped the edge of the table, her knuckles white, her jaw tight. "What do you mean?" she demanded. "What are you trying to say?"

John sighed, running a hand through his hair. He looked tired—bone-deep tired in a way she had never seen before. "I mean, maybe we need to start thinking about other options," he said carefully. "Adoption, surrogacy... or maybe—"

"Or maybe what?" she snapped, cutting him off. Her voice had risen, sharp and defensive. "Maybe we just give up? Is that what you're saying?"

"I'm saying we can't keep doing this to ourselves," John said, his voice strained. "The appointments, the treatments, the disappointment every month—it's destroying us, Mary."

"It's destroying you," she spat, her anger bubbling to the surface. "You're the one who's ready to give up, not me."

John flinched, his lips pressing into a thin line. He looked down at his coffee mug, his shoulders slumping. "This isn't about giving up," he said quietly. "It's about moving forward."

"Moving forward?" Mary's laugh was bitter and hollow. "You mean moving on. From me. From us."

"That's not what I said."

"It's what you meant."

John looked up then, his eyes meeting hers. For a moment, she thought she saw something flicker there—regret, maybe, or guilt. But it was gone as quickly as it came, replaced by a hard, unyielding resolve.

"I can't do this anymore," he said simply.

Mary felt the ground shift beneath her, her world tilting on its axis. She opened her mouth to argue, to plead, but no words came out. The silence between them was deafening.

The memory blurred, shifting to another day, another fight. This one had been worse. Louder. More vicious. John had come home late, the smell of alcohol on his breath, his tie loosened and his hair dishevelled. She had been waiting for him in the living room, her arms crossed, her foot tapping against the floor.

"Where were you?" she demanded as he walked through the door.

"Out," he said flatly, not meeting her eyes.

"With who?" she pressed, her voice rising. "Don't lie to me, John."

"It doesn't matter," he snapped, his tone sharp enough to cut. "I needed a break, okay? From you, from this—" He gestured vaguely around the room. "From everything."

Mary had stared at him, her heart pounding in her chest. "A break?" she echoed. "From me? I'm your wife, John. We're supposed to be in this together."

"Together?" John laughed bitterly, shaking his head. "We stopped being 'together' a long time ago, Mary. All we do is fight. All we do is hurt each other."

"You think I want to fight with you?" she shouted, tears streaming down her face. "You think I want to feel like this every day?"

"Then maybe we should stop pretending this is working," he shot back, his voice cold and hard. "Maybe we should stop pretending we can fix this."

The words hung in the air, heavy and final. Mary felt her knees weaken, her breath catching in her throat. "You don't mean that," she whispered. "You don't."

John didn't respond. He just looked at her, his expression unreadable, and walked away.

The rain outside grew heavier, the sound intensifying as Mary's thoughts spiralled further into the past. She remembered the day he left, the way he had stood in the doorway with his suitcase in hand, his face a mask of indifference.

"I'm sorry," he had said, though his tone lacked any real remorse. "But I can't stay here anymore."

She had begged him to stay, clinging to him like a drowning woman clings to a life raft. But he had pulled away, his hands gentle but firm, and walked out the door without looking back.

Mary had stood there for hours, staring at the empty driveway, waiting for him to change his mind. But he never came back.

The memory shifted again, this time to the days and weeks that followed. The house had felt unbearably empty without him, every room echoing with his absence. Mary had thrown herself into cleaning, scrubbing every surface until her hands were raw and her knees ached. She had rearranged the furniture, redecorated the bedroom, anything to make the house feel different.

But it hadn't helped. The silence remained, a constant reminder of everything she had lost.

It was during that time that the children had come into her life. Emily and Daniel had started as a faint idea, a daydream she clung to during her darkest moments. She imagined their laughter filling the house, their little feet pattering against the floor, their drawings hanging on the fridge.

At first, it was just a coping mechanism, a way to fill the void left by her husband's departure. But over time, the line between fantasy and reality began to blur. The children became more real to her than the pain, more real than the memories of John.

"They're all I need," Mary whispered to herself, her voice trembling. "They're my family now."

The rain began to taper off, the steady rhythm fading into a soft drizzle. Mary stood from the armchair, her legs stiff and unsteady. She moved to the mantle, where the children's drawings were displayed in their mismatched frames.

She traced her fingers over one of the pictures—a crayon drawing of a house with smoke curling from the chimney and a bright yellow sun in the sky. Three stick figures stood in front of the house, their hands joined: one labelled *Mummy,* one labelled *Emily,* and one labelled *Daniel.*

"They're real," she said aloud, her voice firm. "They're real, and they need me."

The house was silent, but Mary didn't feel alone. She could feel their presence, hear their laughter, see their smiles. And that was all that mattered.

Mary turned away from the mantle, her thoughts shifting back to Jemma. The memory of her smiling face, her perfect family, her effortless happiness, burnt in Mary's mind like a brand.

"She doesn't know what it's like to lose everything," Mary muttered, her jaw tightening. "She doesn't know what it's like to have nothing."

Her fists clenched at her sides, her nails digging into her palms. "She's going to understand," she whispered. "They're all going to understand."

Her reflection in the window caught her eye, and for a moment, she didn't recognise the woman staring back at her. The eyes were too dark, too hollow, and the expression was one of pure hatred.

But Mary didn't look away. She couldn't.

"They'll see," she said, her voice steady and cold. "They'll all see."

Chapter 7
The First Kill

Mary stood by the window in her living room, staring out into the quiet night. The street was bathed in the faint orange glow of streetlights, the occasional rustle of leaves breaking the silence. Her breathing was slow, deliberate, as if she were trying to steady herself for what was to come.

Jemma's house was just a few blocks away. She had been there earlier that evening, parked across the street, watching. It had become her ritual—a nightly pilgrimage to observe Jemma's perfect life. The curtains were drawn, but Mary had seen the shadows of Jemma and her husband moving through the living room. The laughter that carried faintly through the walls haunted her even now.

"She doesn't deserve it," Mary whispered, her voice trembling with anger. "She doesn't deserve any of it."

Her fists clenched at her sides, her nails digging into her palms. The thought of Jemma's perfect smile, her flawless family, the effortless joy that radiated from her—it was too much. It made Mary's chest tighten with a mix of rage and despair.

The children were asleep upstairs, as they always were when Mary went out. She had kissed them goodnight, tucking

Emily's stuffed bear under her arm and smoothing Daniel's blanket over his small frame. They were safe here. They always would be.

"I'll be back soon," she had whispered before closing the door quietly behind her.

Mary grabbed her coat from the back of the chair, slipping it on with mechanical precision. Her movements were automatic, her mind racing ahead to what lay before her. She checked her pocket for the list she had folded earlier, her fingers brushing against the rough paper. Jemma's name was at the top, bold and underlined.

She left the house, locking the door behind her, and walked to her car. The night air was crisp, the faint scent of rain lingering from the afternoon's downpour. She slid into the driver's seat, her hands gripping the steering wheel tightly as she started the engine.

The drive to Jemma's house was short but felt longer than usual. Mary's mind buzzed with a thousand thoughts, her heart pounding in her chest. She pictured Jemma's face, the way she had smiled so confidently during the charity event, the way she had cradled her child with such ease. That image had haunted Mary for days, replaying in her mind like a broken record.

The car came to a stop a few houses down from Jemma's. Mary turned off the engine and sat in silence for a moment, staring at the house. The porch light was on, casting a warm glow across the front yard. The curtains in the living room were drawn, but the faint flicker of a television screen was visible through the fabric.

Mary exhaled slowly, her breath fogging up the window. Her hands trembled as she reached for the door handle, her mind screaming at her to stop, to go home, to forget this madness. But the anger inside her was louder, drowning out the voice of reason.

She stepped out of the car, closing the door softly behind her. The street was quiet, the only sound the distant hum of crickets. Mary's footsteps were nearly silent as she approached the house, her coat billowing slightly in the breeze.

Jemma's garden was just as perfect as the rest of her life. The flowerbeds were meticulously maintained, vibrant blooms adding pops of colour to the otherwise dark night. Mary's lip curled as she crouched near the side of the house, her eyes scanning the windows for any sign of movement.

The living room light flickered off, plunging the house into darkness. Mary's heart quickened. She waited, her breaths shallow, as she watched the upstairs windows. One by one, the lights went out, signalling that the family had gone to bed.

Mary stood slowly, her muscles tense. She crept toward the back of the house, her movements deliberate and cautious. The back door was locked, as she had expected, but the garden tools leaning against the shed gave her an idea. She grabbed a small spade, its cold metal handle sending a chill through her fingers, and used it to pry the latch open.

The door swung inward with a soft creak. Mary froze, holding her breath as she listened for any sound from inside the house. When none came, she stepped inside, closing the door gently behind her.

The kitchen was immaculate, the countertops gleaming under the faint light from the window. Mary's gaze swept over the room, taking in the neatly arranged dishes, the perfectly aligned appliances. Everything about this house screamed perfection, and it made her stomach churn.

She moved quietly through the house, her footsteps light against the tiled floor. The staircase loomed ahead, its steps carpeted and muffling her movements as she ascended. Her heart pounded in her ears, her breaths shallow and rapid.

At the top of the stairs, she paused, her hand gripping the railing tightly. The hallway was dark, the doors closed. Mary's eyes adjusted slowly, her gaze landing on the door at the end of the hall. She knew instinctively it was the master bedroom.

She approached the door, her hand trembling as she reached for the handle. It turned easily, the door swinging open with a faint creak. Jemma was asleep in the bed, her face serene in the dim light filtering through the curtains. Her husband lay beside her, his back turned toward the door.

Mary stepped inside, her movements slow and deliberate. She pulled a knife from her pocket, the blade catching the faint light and glinting ominously. Her hands shook as she gripped the handle, her mind racing with a mix of fear and determination.

Jemma stirred slightly, her brow furrowing as if sensing the presence in the room. Mary froze, her breath catching in her throat. But after a moment, Jemma's breathing evened out again, and Mary exhaled slowly.

She moved closer, her footsteps silent against the carpet. The anger inside her burnt hot and bright, fuelling her as she raised the knife.

"This is for everything I've lost," she whispered, her voice barely audible. "For everything you took from me."

Jemma's eyes fluttered open, her expression shifting from confusion to terror as she saw Mary standing over her. She opened her mouth to scream, but Mary's hand was faster, pressing down hard against her throat as the knife sliced across it in a swift, brutal motion.

The room erupted into chaos. Jemma's husband shot up from the bed, his eyes wide with shock, but Mary was already moving. She shoved him hard, sending him sprawling to the floor. He scrambled backward, his hands raised in a gesture of surrender.

"Stay down," Mary hissed, her voice low and venomous. "Don't make me do it to you too."

The man's chest heaved as he stared at her, his face pale with fear. Mary turned back to Jemma, her chest tight as she looked down at the lifeless body. Blood pooled on the white sheets, its metallic scent filling the room. She didn't feel the satisfaction she had expected. Instead, there was a strange emptiness, a hollow ache that gnawed at her insides.

She didn't have time to dwell on it. She turned and fled the room, her footsteps pounding against the stairs as she raced toward the back door. The spade she had used to break in lay forgotten on the counter as she slipped outside, disappearing into the night.

When Mary returned home, the house was quiet and still. She locked the door behind her and leaned against it, her chest heaving as she caught her breath. Her hands were stained with blood, her coat splattered with dark, sticky patches.

She climbed the stairs slowly, her legs trembling beneath her. The children's room was just as she had left it, the faint glow of the nightlight casting soft shadows on the walls. Mary stepped inside, her gaze falling on the two neatly made beds.

"I'm home," she whispered, her voice trembling. "Mummy's home."

She sat on the edge of Emily's bed, her hands shaking as she reached for the stuffed bear. She clutched it tightly to her chest, tears streaming down her face.

"I did it for you," she whispered, her voice breaking. "I did it all for you."

The house remained silent, the only sound the faint rustle of the wind outside. But Mary didn't feel alone. She never felt alone. Not when her children were here.

Chapter 8
A Fragile Normalcy

Mary sat at the kitchen table, her hands wrapped around a mug of tea that had long since gone cold. The house was silent, the only sounds the faint hum of the refrigerator and the occasional groan of the floorboards settling. She stared at the clock on the wall, watching the second-hand tick steadily forward. It was almost 7:00 a.m.—time to wake the children.

Her hands trembled as she set the mug down, the faint clink of ceramic against wood startling her in the quiet. She wiped her palms against her skirt, trying to steady herself. The events of the night before felt like a distant dream, hazy and unreal. But the dark stains on her coat, which she had stuffed into the back of her closet, told a different story.

"It's a new day," Mary said aloud, her voice shaky but resolute. "They need me to hold it together."

She stood and smoothed her skirt, her movements deliberate as she forced herself into her routine. Breakfast had to be made. The children would be hungry.

The familiar rhythm of cracking eggs and slicing toast grounded her, the mechanical motions offering a sense of normalcy she desperately needed. She plated the food carefully—scrambled eggs and toast for Daniel, a smaller portion with jam for Emily. She poured two glasses of milk and placed them beside the plates, stepping back to inspect her work.

"Perfect," she whispered, her lips curving into a faint smile. She glanced toward the staircase. "Emily, Daniel, time to get up! Breakfast is ready!"

The silence that followed was heavier than usual, pressing against her like a weight. Mary frowned, her chest tightening. She moved to the foot of the stairs, calling again. "I mean it! Get up, or you'll be late!"

Her voice echoed in the empty house. Mary waited a moment longer before sighing and returning to the kitchen. "They'll come down when they're ready," she muttered, sitting down at the table.

She watched the clock tick forward, her appetite non-existent as the eggs on her plate grew cold. The memories of the night before crept into her mind, unbidden and unwelcome. The image of Jemma's lifeless body flashed behind her eyes, the blood pooling on the white sheets, the metallic scent filling the room.

Mary clenched her fists, her nails digging into her palms. "It had to be done," she said under her breath. "She didn't deserve it. She didn't deserve any of it."

The words felt hollow, even as she repeated them. She forced herself to eat a bite of toast, the dry bread sticking to the roof of her mouth. She washed it down with a sip of tea, the lukewarm liquid making her stomach churn.

After breakfast, Mary threw herself into cleaning. She scrubbed the counters until they gleamed, vacuumed the living room carpet, and dusted every surface she could reach.

The physical labour kept her mind occupied, the repetitive motions soothing in their simplicity.

She avoided the closet where her coat lay, the memory of its dark stains too fresh, too raw. Instead, she focused on the tasks at hand, moving from room to room with mechanical precision.

When she reached the children's room, she paused in the doorway, her heart constricting. The beds were neatly made, the toys arranged just as she had left them. She stepped inside, her footsteps soft against the carpet.

"Emily, Daniel," she said softly, her voice trembling. "Are you doing your lessons?"

The room remained silent, the faint hum of the nightlight the only sound. Mary's gaze fell on Daniel's desk, where his math workbook lay closed. She crossed the room, her fingers brushing against the cover.

"You didn't finish your assignment," she murmured, her tone a mix of reprimand and sadness. "You know how important it is to stay on top of your work."

She opened the workbook, flipping through the blank pages. Her chest ached as she traced the faint outline of the pencil marks she had made herself, the ghost of an attempt to keep the illusion alive.

"You'll do better tomorrow," she said, closing the workbook and setting it neatly back in place. "I know you will."

Mary moved to Emily's bed, picking up the stuffed bear that sat propped against the pillow. She held it close, her tears soaking into its worn fabric. "I love you both so much," she whispered. "Everything I do is for you."

The rest of the day passed in a blur. Mary moved through her routines mechanically, her mind a storm of conflicting emotions. She wanted to believe that what she had done was justified, that it had been necessary. But the doubt lingered, gnawing at the edges of her resolve.

By mid-afternoon, the local news had begun reporting on Jemma's murder. Mary sat on the couch, her hands folded tightly in her lap, as the anchor-woman detailed the gruesome discovery.

"The body of Jemma Theaker, a beloved member of the community, was found early this morning in her home," the anchor said, her tone somber. "Authorities believe the attack occurred late last night. Police are asking anyone with information to come forward."

Mary's stomach churned as the screen cut to footage of Jemma's house, the yard cordoned off with yellow tape. A police officer stood near the front door, speaking to a reporter. The sight of the house—the place she had been less than twenty-four hours ago—sent a chill down her spine.

She reached for the remote and turned off the television, unable to watch any longer. Her chest heaved as she tried to steady her breathing, her hands trembling in her lap.

"They don't know it was me," she whispered. "They can't know."

Her mind raced with thoughts of what she should do next. She couldn't let herself spiral. The children needed her to stay strong.

As evening approached, Mary prepared dinner, her movements slow and deliberate. She set the table for three, placing the plates and glasses with careful precision. The sight of the empty chairs across from her made her chest ache, but she pushed the feeling aside.

"Emily, Daniel, dinner's ready!" she called, her voice bright and cheerful.

She sat at the table, folding her hands neatly in her lap as she waited. The seconds ticked by, the silence stretching longer with each passing moment. Her gaze drifted to the empty chairs, her throat tightening.

"You're not going to make me eat alone, are you?" she asked softly, her voice trembling. "You know how much I hate that."

When no response came, Mary forced herself to eat a few bites of her food. The taste was bland, the texture unappealing, but she swallowed it down anyway. She couldn't let herself fall apart. Not now.

After dinner, she cleaned the dishes and wiped down the table, her mind racing with thoughts she couldn't quiet. The image of Jemma's lifeless body haunted her, a constant presence in the back of her mind.

"She deserved it," Mary whispered, her voice firm. "She didn't appreciate what she had. None of them do."

But even as she said the words, a flicker of doubt lingered. What if the police found her? What if they came to her door, asking questions she couldn't answer?

Mary shook her head, her jaw tightening. "They won't," she said aloud. "They can't."

That night, as she lay in bed, Mary stared at the ceiling, her thoughts swirling. The whispers had started again, faint and indistinct, like a breeze rustling through the trees.

"She had it coming," they said. "She didn't deserve her happiness."

Mary closed her eyes, her chest tightening. The whispers were right, she told herself. Jemma had been too perfect, too happy. She hadn't known what it was like to suffer, to lose everything.

But as the hours dragged on and sleep eluded her, the doubt began to creep in once more. The whispers grew louder, more insistent, until they filled her mind completely.

"You did the right thing," they said. "You're making the world better."

Mary clung to the words like a lifeline, repeating them over and over in her mind. She had done the right thing. She had to believe that.

As the first light of dawn began to filter through the curtains, Mary finally drifted off to sleep, her body heavy with exhaustion. But even in her dreams, she couldn't escape the memory of what she had done. Jemma's face followed her, a ghost she couldn't outrun.

Chapter 9
Cracks in the Facade

The sun rose reluctantly, casting weak, pale light over Mary's small house. She stood at the kitchen sink, staring out at the overgrown garden while her hands moved mechanically, scrubbing a plate that no longer needed cleaning. Her reflection in the window stared back at her, its eyes hollow and unfocused. She paused for a moment, her hands still submerged in soapy water, and let out a long breath.

The whispers had started earlier that morning, faint and elusive, just as they always were. They circled the edges of her mind, sometimes teasing, sometimes accusing, but always there. She had tried to ignore them, throwing herself into her chores, but their presence gnawed at her like a splinter she couldn't remove.

"They know," one of them hissed, the voice low and guttural.

"No, they don't," she whispered back, her voice barely audible. She gripped the plate tighter, her knuckles turning white. "Nobody knows. Nobody saw me."

"Are you sure?" another voice taunted, this one higher, sharper. "They're talking about you. Watching you."

Mary shook her head violently, drops of water flying from her hands as she slammed the plate onto the drying rack. "You're not real," she said through clenched teeth. "You don't know anything."

The whispers subsided briefly, retreating into the shadows of her mind, but the unease they left behind lingered. Mary turned away from the sink, wiping her hands on a dish towel as she glanced at the clock. It was nearly 8:30 a.m.

"Time to get moving," she muttered to herself, the words feeling more like a command than a statement.

Breakfast was the same as always: scrambled eggs, toast, and milk. Mary prepared the plates with her usual precision, setting them on the table in their designated spots. She called for the children twice, her voice carrying up the stairs, but the silence that followed felt heavier than usual.

"Emily, Daniel!" she called again, her tone sharper. "If you don't come down now, there won't be anything left for you."

She sat at the table, her eyes fixed on the two empty chairs across from her. Her fingers tapped a restless rhythm against the wood as she waited. The seconds dragged on, each one feeling longer than the last.

"They're ungrateful," the whispers said, creeping back into her thoughts. "You do so much for them, and they ignore you."

Mary's jaw tightened, her hands curling into fists. "They're just children," she said softly. "They don't know any better."

But the anger simmering beneath the surface refused to be quelled. She stood abruptly, her chair scraping loudly against the floor as she grabbed the plates and dumped their contents into the trash. "If you're not going to eat, then you can go hungry," she muttered, her voice shaking.

After breakfast, Mary busied herself with cleaning, hoping the physical labour would drown out the thoughts that plagued her. She scrubbed the counters until her hands were raw, vacuumed the carpet in precise, straight lines, and dusted every surface she could reach. But no matter how hard she worked, she couldn't shake the feeling that something was wrong.

The news of Jemma's murder had spread quickly, and the neighbourhood buzzed with speculation. Mary had overheard snippets of conversation from the neighbours as she had taken out the trash that morning. Their words had been quiet, their voices hushed, but Mary had caught enough to know they were afraid.

"Did you hear what happened to Jemma?" one woman had whispered.

"Awful," another replied. "And so close to home. I can't even imagine."

Mary had hurried back inside before she could hear more, her chest tight with unease. She couldn't help but feel their eyes on her, watching her, judging her.

"They're suspicious," the whispers said, louder now. "They know it was you."

"No, they don't," Mary snapped, slamming the vacuum cleaner against the wall as she turned it off. Her breaths came in short, shallow bursts as she pressed her back against the nearest surface, trying to calm herself. "They can't know."

But the doubt lingered, coiling around her like a snake.

By the time lunch rolled around, Mary's nerves were frayed. She sat at the table, picking at a sandwich she had made for herself, the children's plates sitting untouched in front of their empty chairs. She glanced toward the window, her gaze flickering to the house across the street.

Her neighbour, a middle-aged woman named Mrs. Turner, was standing on her front porch, her arms crossed as she watched two teenagers unload groceries from the trunk of a car. Her face was pinched with disapproval, her lips pursed as she barked instructions at the boys.

Mary's stomach twisted at the sight of her. She had always disliked Mrs. Turner, with her nosy tendencies and judgemental stares. The woman had made it clear from the day Mary moved in that she didn't approve of her.

"She's probably talking about you right now," the whispers said.

Mary's grip on her fork tightened, her knuckles turning white. "Let her talk," she muttered. "She doesn't know anything about me."

But the thought of Mrs. Turner gossiping about her, spreading rumours to the rest of the neighbourhood, made her blood boil.

"She thinks she's better than you," the whispers added, their tone insidious. "She always has."

Mary pushed her plate away, her appetite gone. She stood and walked to the window, pulling the curtain aside just enough to peek out. Mrs. Turner was still on the porch, her arms now gesturing wildly as she scolded one of the teenagers.

Mary's jaw tightened. She didn't have to put up with this—not from Mrs. Turner, not from anyone.

The rest of the day passed in a blur. Mary moved through her routine with mechanical precision, her mind racing with thoughts she couldn't quiet. The whispers came and went, their voices like an itch she couldn't scratch.

"They're all watching you," they said. "Waiting for you to slip up."

Mary shook her head, trying to silence them, but their words lingered, burrowing into her thoughts. By the time evening rolled around, she felt like she was coming apart at the seams.

She sat on the couch, staring blankly at the television as the local news played in the background. The anchor was discussing Jemma's murder again, the headline flashing across the bottom of the screen: **"Local Mother Found Murdered in Home—Police Investigating."**

Mary's chest tightened as she listened to the report. The police had no suspects, but they were urging anyone with information to come forward. A photo of Jemma appeared on the screen, her smiling face a stark contrast to the grim news.

"She's gone," Mary whispered, her voice hollow. "She's really gone."

The realisation hit her like a tidal wave, leaving her breathless. She had done this. She had taken someone's life.

And she wasn't sure she could stop.

As the night deepened, the whispers grew louder, more insistent. Mary paced the living room, her hands wringing together as she tried to block them out. But their words seeped into her mind, twisting her thoughts into something dark and unrecognisable.

"You're doing the right thing," they said. "They deserve this. All of them."

Mary stopped in her tracks, her chest heaving as she stared at her reflection in the window. The woman staring back at her looked like a stranger—her eyes were wild, her hair dishevelled, her face pale and drawn.

"I don't know if I can do this," she whispered, her voice trembling.

The whispers didn't respond.

When she finally climbed the stairs to bed, Mary paused outside the children's room. She pushed the door open slowly, her gaze falling on the two neatly made beds. The sight of them brought a small sense of comfort, a reminder of why she was doing this.

"I'm protecting you," she said softly, her voice barely audible. "I'm doing it all for you."

She stepped inside and sat on the edge of Daniel's bed, her hand resting on the blanket. The room was quiet, the faint hum of the nightlight the only sound.

"They don't understand," she whispered, her voice breaking. "But they will. They'll all understand."

The silence pressed in around her, heavy and suffocating, but Mary didn't feel alone. Not here. Not with her children.

Chapter 10
The Second Kill

The world outside Mary's window was deceptively serene. The sun hung low in the sky, casting a warm, golden glow over the neighbourhood. Children's laughter echoed faintly as they played in the distance, their voices carrying on the gentle breeze. To anyone else, it might have seemed like an idyllic afternoon. But to Mary, it was a reminder of everything she didn't have—everything she could never have.

She sat on the edge of her couch, staring out the window with unblinking eyes. The whispers had been relentless all morning, their voices weaving through her thoughts like a poison. They whispered of betrayal, of judgement, of eyes that watched her every move. She felt exposed, vulnerable, as if the entire neighbourhood knew what she had done.

"They're laughing at you," one voice hissed. "They think you're pathetic."

Mary's hands clenched into fists, her nails digging into her palms. "They don't know anything," she muttered under her breath.

"They're waiting for you to slip up," another voice added, sharp and mocking. "They're just like her."

Her jaw tightened. She didn't need to ask who *her* was. Jemma's face flashed in her mind, her perfect smile and perfect life, now gone. Mary had made sure of that. But it hadn't been enough. The anger, the jealousy—it still burnt inside her, consuming her like a fire that refused to be extinguished.

She stood abruptly, her chest heaving as she tried to steady her breathing. "I need to get out of here," she said to herself. "Just for a little while."

Mary grabbed her coat from the hook by the door and slipped it on, the fabric still carrying the faint, metallic scent of blood. She had scrubbed it as best she could, but the stains were stubborn, refusing to disappear entirely. She shoved the thought aside as she stepped outside, locking the door behind her. The children were safe, tucked away in their room, just as they always were when she went out.

The air was cool and crisp, carrying with it the scent of freshly cut grass. Mary walked briskly down the sidewalk, her eyes darting to the houses she passed. Curtains fluttered as neighbours peeked out, their eyes lingering on her for just a moment too long before disappearing from view. At least, that's how it felt to Mary. She could feel their judgement, their suspicion, like a weight pressing down on her.

"They know," the whispers said, their voices crawling into her ears. "They're watching you."

Mary shook her head, her pace quickening. She didn't know where she was going, only that she needed to get away. Her feet carried her to the park, a place she had avoided for weeks. The sight of happy families, of mothers doting on their children, had always been too much to bear. But today, she felt drawn to it, as if the anger inside her needed fuel.

The park was bustling with activity. Children ran across the grass, their laughter piercing the air. Mothers gathered in small groups, chatting and sipping coffee from travel mugs. Mary lingered near the entrance, her eyes scanning the scene. The sight of them—so carefree, so content—made her stomach churn.

Her gaze settled on a woman sitting alone on a bench near the playground. She had a baby stroller parked beside her, its occupant gurgling happily as the woman adjusted a toy hanging from the canopy. She looked young, perhaps in her late twenties, with dark hair pulled into a loose ponytail and a serene expression on her face.

Mary's chest tightened as she watched her. There was something about the woman's calm demeanour, her effortless smile, that ignited a spark of rage within her. She had seen that look before—on Jemma's face, on the faces of so many others. It was a look of contentment, of security, of a life untouched by pain.

"She's just like the rest of them," the whispers said, their voices dripping with disdain. "She doesn't know what it's like to suffer."

Mary's hands curled into fists at her sides. The whispers were right. This woman didn't know what it was like to lose everything, to be left with nothing but the echoes of a life she had dreamed of but could never have. She didn't deserve her happiness.

Without realising it, Mary began to move toward the bench. Her steps were slow, deliberate, her mind focused entirely on the woman. The whispers grew louder, their voices urging her forward, drowning out any lingering doubts.

Excuse me," Mary said, her voice soft but firm. The woman looked up, startled, her serene expression faltering for a moment.

"Yes?" the woman replied, her tone polite but cautious.

Mary forced a smile, though it didn't reach her eyes. "I couldn't help but notice how adorable your baby is," she said, nodding toward the stroller.

The woman's expression softened, her guard lowering slightly. "Oh, thank you," she said, glancing at her child with a smile. "He's a handful, but he's worth it."

"I'm sure he is," Mary said, her voice tight. She could feel the anger bubbling beneath the surface, threatening to spill over. "It must be nice, having a family like this."

The woman looked at her more closely now, her brow furrowing slightly. "It is," she said carefully. "I feel very lucky."

Mary's smile faded, her hands trembling at her sides. "Lucky," she repeated, her voice dripping with bitterness. "You have no idea how lucky you are."

The woman's smile faltered, her eyes narrowing slightly. "I'm sorry," she said slowly. "Do I know you?"

"No," Mary said, her voice flat. "But you remind me of someone."

Before the woman could respond, Mary's hand shot out, gripping her wrist with surprising force. The woman gasped, her eyes widening in shock as she tried to pull away.

"Let go of me!" she cried, her voice rising in panic.

Mary's mind was a blur of rage and desperation. The whispers screamed in her ears, their voices a cacophony of hatred and anger. She didn't think—she couldn't. Her free hand reached into her pocket, closing around the knife she had brought with her. She pulled it out in one swift motion, the blade catching the sunlight as it arced through the air.

The woman's scream was cut short as the knife found its mark, slashing across her throat with brutal precision. Blood spilt onto the bench, pooling beneath the woman as her body went limp. Mary stepped back, her chest heaving as she stared at the lifeless figure before her.

The whispers fell silent, leaving only the sound of her ragged breathing and the faint cries of the baby in the stroller. Mary's hands were slick with blood, the knife trembling in her grasp.

"She deserved it," she whispered, her voice barely audible. "They all do."

Mary fled the scene, her heart pounding in her chest as she weaved through the neighbourhood. She didn't look back, didn't stop until she reached her house. She fumbled with the keys, her bloodied hands making it difficult to unlock the door. When she finally stepped inside, she collapsed against the wall, her body shaking with a mixture of adrenaline and exhaustion.

The house was silent, the faint hum of the refrigerator the only sound. Mary sank to the floor, the knife slipping from her grasp and clattering against the wood. Her hands trembled as she stared at the blood smeared across her fingers, the reality of what she had done sinking in.

But as the minutes passed, the guilt began to fade, replaced by a twisted sense of satisfaction. She had done what needed to be done. She had taken another step toward making the world understand her pain.

"They'll see," she whispered, her voice steady. "They'll all see."

Mary pushed herself to her feet, her legs unsteady but determined. She moved to the sink, washing her hands with mechanical precision, scrubbing away the blood until her skin was raw. The whispers began to stir again, faint and soothing now, their tone almost approving.

"You're doing the right thing," they said. "Keep going."

Mary nodded to herself, her resolve hardening. She wasn't done—not yet.

Chapter 11
A Friendly Stranger

The grocery store was unusually busy for a Wednesday afternoon, with shoppers weaving through the aisles like ants in a colony. Mary gripped the handle of her cart, her knuckles white as she navigated through the crowd. Her list was short—milk, bread, and a few cans of soup—but even these small errands felt overwhelming today. Every step she took seemed magnified, every glance from a stranger heavy with suspicion.

"They know," the whispers murmured, their voices slithering through her thoughts. "They're all looking at you."

Mary shook her head, trying to silence them. "Nobody knows," she muttered under her breath. "Just focus on the list."

But her efforts to block out the whispers were futile. The faces around her blurred together, their expressions unreadable but piercing. A young mother with a toddler in her cart smiled briefly as they passed, but to Mary, it felt mocking. Her chest tightened, and she averted her gaze, focusing on the polished floor tiles beneath her feet.

She turned into the bread aisle, trying to steady her breathing. The voices continued their assault.

"Why are you even here? You don't belong. You never belonged."

Her hands trembled as she reached for a loaf of bread, her grip tightening around the plastic packaging as if it were a lifeline. She needed to finish quickly and get home. The children were waiting for her, and the outside world was closing in too fast.

Mary turned to place the bread in her cart but froze when her elbow knocked into something—or someone. A sharp clatter of metal followed, and she looked down to see a stack of cans rolling across the floor.

"Oh no, I'm so sorry," Mary said quickly, crouching to pick up the cans. Her words felt mechanical, as though spoken by someone else.

"No harm done," a man's voice replied, warm and forgiving. "Happens to the best of us."

Mary glanced up, startled. The man crouched beside her, reaching for a car that had rolled under the shelf. His brown hair was slightly dishevelled, his face clean-shaven and open, with a soft smile that didn't carry the weight of judgement she had come to expect.

She blinked, unsure of how to respond. "I didn't mean to—" she began, but the words caught in her throat.

"It's fine, really," he said, handing her the last can. His eyes met hers, and for the first time in what felt like years, Mary didn't feel scrutinised. There was something disarming about him, something... kind.

"I—thank you," she stammered, standing and placing the cans back in her cart.

"Anytime," he said, straightening. His voice carried an ease that felt foreign to her, as though he belonged in a world she hadn't touched in years. "You looked like you had a lot on your mind. Happens to me all the time."

Mary hesitated, unsure of what to say. She wasn't used to small talk anymore, not after so many years of keeping to herself. But his demeanour was genuine, not forced, and it stirred something in her she hadn't felt in a long time—a faint flicker of connection.

"It's been… a long week," she admitted, her voice quieter than she intended.

He nodded as though he understood completely. "Haven't we all had those? I'm Thomas, by the way." He extended his hand, his smile warm and inviting.

Mary hesitated before taking it, her fingers brushing against his briefly before she pulled away. "Mary," she said simply.

"Nice to meet you, Mary," Thomas said, his voice still kind. "Well, if you need help knocking over more cans, you know where to find me." He chuckled softly, a sound that felt strangely comforting.

Mary allowed herself a small smile, though it felt foreign on her face. "I'll try to keep it under control," she replied, her tone faintly teasing.

Thomas gave her a slight nod before pushing his cart down the aisle, disappearing around the corner. Mary watched him go, her heart pounding in her chest. It wasn't fear or anger she felt, but something far more unsettling—hope.

The rest of her shopping trip passed in a haze. The whispers in her mind were quieter now, their incessant accusations drowned out by the memory of Thomas's voice. It had been so long since someone had spoken to her without judgement, without pity. She replayed their conversation in her mind, clinging to it as she loaded her groceries into the car and drove home.

As she pulled into her driveway, Mary's thoughts drifted to the children. Would they like Thomas? Would he understand how special they were, how much they meant to her? The idea was absurd, of course—she had only just met him. But the thought lingered, planting a seed of possibility in her mind.

Later that evening, Mary sat at the kitchen table, staring at the empty plates she had set for Emily and Daniel. She had made their favourite—macaroni and cheese with little pieces of hot dog mixed in—but the sight of the untouched food only deepened the ache in her chest.

"I met someone today," she said aloud, her voice breaking the heavy silence. "His name is Thomas."

The room remained still, the faint hum of the refrigerator the only sound. Mary picked up her fork, twirling it absently in her fingers as she continued. "He seems nice. Kind. The kind of person who might… understand."

Her words felt strange, as though she were speaking them into a void. But the presence of her children, invisible though it was, gave her the courage to keep going.

"I think he'd like you," she said softly, glancing at the empty chairs. "Maybe one day, I'll introduce you."

The idea both terrified and exhilarated her. She had kept the children hidden from the world for so long, protecting them from prying eyes and cruel judgements. But Thomas… he was different. She could feel it in the way he had looked at her, in the sincerity of his smile.

As the days passed, Mary found herself thinking about Thomas more often than she cared to admit. She began visiting the grocery store at odd hours, hoping to run into him again. Her errands, which had once been a source of dread, became an opportunity to recapture the fleeting sense of normalcy she had felt in his presence.

When she finally saw him again, it was as though the weight on her chest had lifted, if only slightly. He greeted her with the same warm smile, his eyes lighting up as though he were genuinely pleased to see her.

"Mary," he said, his tone easy and familiar. "How have you been?"

She hesitated for a moment before replying. "Better," she said honestly. "I think."

Thomas nodded, his expression softening. "That's good to hear. Sometimes, all it takes is one small step, you know?"

His words lingered in her mind long after they parted ways. One small step. She wasn't entirely sure what he had meant, but the idea resonated with her in a way she couldn't explain. For the first time in years, she felt as though she had been seen—not as an object of pity or scorn, but as a person.

That night, Mary sat in the children's room, her hands resting on the edge of Daniel's bed. The faint glow of the nightlight cast soft shadows on the walls, and the air was thick with a sense of quiet anticipation.

"I think things are going to change," she said softly, her voice trembling with a mix of hope and fear. "I don't know how, but... I think they will."

The silence that followed was almost comforting, as though the room itself were listening. Mary closed her eyes, letting the thought wash over her like a wave. Change. It was terrifying, but it was also the first thing in a long time that felt real.

As she stood and turned off the light, she whispered one final thought into the darkness: "Maybe we don't have to be alone anymore."

Chapter 12
Protecting the Family

Mary sat at the edge of the children's room, her hands gripping the back of the small wooden chair she had dragged inside. The soft glow of the nightlight illuminated the space, casting long, comforting shadows across the walls. She stared at the two neatly made beds, her eyes darting between Emily's pink quilt and Daniel's blue comforter. Everything was just as it should be. Perfect. Peaceful.

But inside her mind, chaos brewed.

The whispers had returned, more insistent now, warning her of unseen threats. They told her of prying eyes, of people who wanted to take her children away. They painted vivid images of strangers bursting through her front door, their hands reaching for Emily and Daniel, dragging them into the harsh world beyond these walls.

"You can't let them," the whispers urged. "They'll destroy everything."

Mary's hands trembled as she pulled the chair closer to the beds, her body rigid and alert. She couldn't sleep, not when the danger felt so close. The whispers were right. The world outside was full of people who wouldn't understand, who would try to tear apart the family she had worked so hard to build.

"I won't let anyone hurt you," she whispered into the quiet room, her voice trembling but resolute. "Not ever."

The next morning, Mary's exhaustion weighed heavily on her, but she forced herself into her routine. Breakfast came first, as always. She prepared scrambled eggs and toast, arranging the plates with her usual precision. The kitchen was quiet except for the clink of silverware against the ceramic dishes, but Mary spoke as though her children were sitting right in front of her.

"You need to eat all of it today," she said, glancing at the empty chairs. "I don't want to hear any excuses, Daniel. And Emily, no hiding your eggs under the toast. I always know."

The silence stretched on, heavy and oppressive. Mary's hands stilled as a thought crept into her mind, unbidden and unwelcome. What if they weren't safe here? What if someone found out about them?

"They're watching," the whispers said, their voices dripping with malice. "They know."

Mary's chest tightened as she stared at the table, her breathing shallow. She couldn't let that happen. She had to protect her children, no matter what. They were the only thing she had left, the only thing keeping her grounded.

The thought of losing them was unbearable.

Later that day, Mary found herself at the grocery store again, wandering the aisles with no real purpose. She wasn't sure why she had come—there wasn't anything she needed—but the house had felt too small, too suffocating. The whispers had followed her here, but their voices were quieter, drowned out by the hum of fluorescent lights and the murmur of shoppers around her.

As she turned a corner, her cart nearly collided with another. She looked up, startled, to see Thomas Greene smiling at her, his expression warm and familiar.

"Mary," he said, his tone light. "Fancy meeting you here again."

For a moment, she didn't know how to respond. Her mind was still caught in the grip of her paranoia, the whispers warning her to be careful, to trust no one. But Thomas's smile was disarming, his presence like a balm to her frayed nerves.

"Thomas," she said finally, her voice softer than she intended. "It's... good to see you."

"Likewise," he replied, leaning casually against his cart. "How have you been?"

Mary hesitated, unsure how much to reveal. "Busy," she said vaguely, her fingers gripping the handle of her cart. "Taking care of the house. The kids."

Thomas nodded, his expression thoughtful. "That's a lot of work," he said. "You must be a good mum."

The words caught Mary off guard, striking a chord deep within her. No one had ever called her a good mum before. The validation, however small, sent a wave of warmth through her chest.

"I try," she said quietly, her gaze dropping to the floor.

There was a brief pause, then Thomas spoke again. "Do you have a lot of family nearby? Someone to help out?"

Mary stiffened, the warmth in her chest replaced by a flicker of suspicion. "No," she said quickly. "It's just me and the kids."

Thomas raised his hands slightly, as if to show he meant no harm. "I get it," he said. "It's tough doing it all on your own. My sister's a single mum, and I see how much she struggles."

His words eased some of Mary's tension, though the whispers in her mind remained wary. She glanced at him, studying his face. There was no judgement in his expression, no sign of the cruelty she had come to expect from others. If anything, he looked genuinely interested in what she had to say.

For the first time in what felt like years, Mary felt the faint stirrings of connection.

As the days passed, Mary found herself looking forward to her chance encounters with Thomas. Each interaction was brief but meaningful, a small reprieve from the isolation that had become her life. He would ask her how she was doing, compliment her on her perseverance, and even crack the occasional joke to make her smile.

Mary began to imagine a future where Thomas might become part of her world. She pictured him sitting at the kitchen table, sharing a meal with Emily and Daniel, his laughter filling the space that had been so quiet for so long. The idea was both terrifying and exhilarating.

But the whispers were quick to remind her of the dangers.

"He'll ruin everything," they said. "He'll find out about them."

"No," Mary whispered to herself, her voice firm. "He wouldn't do that. He's different."

The whispers laughed, their tone mocking. "You think he cares about you? About them? He'll leave, just like everyone else."

Mary clenched her fists, her nails digging into her palms. She couldn't let that happen. She had to protect her children, no matter what.

One afternoon, Thomas invited her to grab coffee after they ran into each other at the store. Mary hesitated, torn between the fear of stepping outside her comfort zone and the desire to accept his kindness. In the end, she agreed, surprising even herself.

They sat at a small table near the window of a local café, the sunlight streaming in and casting a warm glow over the room. Thomas stirred his coffee absently as he spoke, sharing stories about his work and his family. Mary listened intently, her guard slowly lowering as she allowed herself to enjoy the moment.

"What about you?" Thomas asked, his gaze steady. "What do you do when you're not taking care of the kids?"

Mary faltered, unsure how to answer. "Not much," she admitted, her voice barely above a whisper. "It's hard to find time for myself."

Thomas nodded, his expression sympathetic. "That makes sense. But you deserve a break too, you know."

His words struck a chord, filling her with a mix of gratitude and longing. She hadn't realised how much she needed to hear that; how much she craved the validation he offered so freely.

"Thank you," she said softly, her eyes meeting his. "That means a lot."

Thomas smiled, his warmth disarming. "Anytime, Mary."

That night, as Mary sat in the children's room, she found herself thinking about Thomas. She imagined introducing him to Emily and Daniel, letting him into the world she had kept hidden for so long. But the thought also filled her with dread. What if he didn't understand? What if he tried to take them away?

The whispers returned, their voices dripping with malice. "You can't trust him. He'll destroy everything."

Mary shook her head, trying to silence them. "No," she whispered. "He's different."

But the doubt lingered, gnawing at the edges of her resolve. She knew she couldn't let her guard down, not completely. The world outside was full of threats, and she had to be ready to protect her family at all costs.

As she lay down to sleep, the whispers grew quieter, their voices fading into the background. But their message remained, etched into her mind like a warning.

"Protect them," they said. "No matter what."

Chapter 13
A Mother's Purpose

The sun filtered through the curtains of the children's room, casting faint golden streaks across the walls. Mary stood in the doorway, watching the soft light inch its way across the floor. She held a basket of freshly folded laundry, the smell of fabric softener wafting faintly around her. It was a scene of domestic tranquillity, the kind she had always longed for, but the tension coiled in her chest told a different story.

"Emily, I've brought your clean clothes," she called softly, stepping inside. "And Daniel, I expect you to keep your dresser organised this time. No more cramming things into random drawers."

Her voice carried an edge of sternness, but it was undercut by an unmistakable tenderness. She moved to Emily's bed first, carefully setting a stack of neatly folded shirts on the pillow. The stuffed bear perched against the headboard tilted slightly, and Mary adjusted it until it sat upright.

"There," she murmured, brushing a strand of hair from her face. "That's better."

She turned to Daniel's bed next, setting his clothes down with the same care. Her gaze lingered on the blue comforter, perfectly smooth and untouched. For a moment, her chest ached with a dull, familiar pain.

"Why don't you ever help me with this?" she asked, her tone half-playful, half-scolding. "You're old enough to take responsibility for your things."

The room was silent, as it always was, but Mary pretended not to notice. She pulled open Daniel's dresser and began arranging his clothes, humming softly under her breath. It was a tune she couldn't quite place, something from her childhood, perhaps, or maybe a fragment of a song she'd made up herself.

As the day unfolded, Mary threw herself into her chores with a sense of purpose that bordered on desperation. The whispers in her mind had grown quieter over the past few days, but they lingered at the edges of her thoughts, ready to pounce the moment her resolve faltered. She couldn't let that happen. She had to stay busy, to keep moving, to prove—to herself, to her children—that she was in control.

The kitchen was her next task. Mary scrubbed the counters until they gleamed, the scent of lemon cleaner filling the air. She wiped down the cabinets, rearranged the spice rack, and swept the floor twice for good measure. By the time she was done, her arms ached and her back protested, but she felt a flicker of satisfaction.

"Emily, Daniel," she called, leaning against the counter to catch her breath. "Lunch is ready."

The table was set with meticulous care: two plates of sandwiches cut into triangles, two glasses of milk, and a small bowl of apple slices in the centre. Mary sat at the head of the table, her eyes flicking between the two empty chairs. The silence pressed against her like a weight, but she forced herself to smile.

"You'll love this," she said brightly, her voice filling the void. "I even remembered to cut the crusts off, just the way you like."

She picked at her own sandwich, her appetite nonexistent. The food felt like sawdust in her mouth, but she forced herself to chew and swallow. She had to set a good example for the children, even if they weren't eating.

As the afternoon wore on, Mary found herself pacing the living room, her mind racing with thoughts she couldn't quiet. She couldn't shake the feeling that she wasn't doing enough, that she wasn't the mother her children deserved. The whispers, faint but persistent, fed her insecurities.

"They need more from you," they said. "You're failing them."

Mary's hands trembled as she clutched the edge of the couch, her nails digging into the fabric. "I'm doing my best," she muttered, her voice shaking. "They know that."

"Do they?" the whispers taunted. "They deserve more. Better."

Tears pricked at Mary's eyes as she sank onto the couch, her head in her hands. She had tried so hard to create a life for her children, to protect them from the cruelty of the outside world. But it never felt like enough. The doubt gnawed at her, threatening to unravel everything she had built.

Her thoughts drifted to Thomas, and a small, fragile hope flickered in her chest. He had been kind to her, understanding in a way she hadn't expected. Perhaps he could help her, could be the stability she so desperately needed.

But the whispers were quick to extinguish that hope.

"He'll take them away," they warned. "He doesn't understand. He'll ruin everything."

Mary shook her head, her tears spilling onto her cheeks. "No," she whispered. "He wouldn't do that. He's different."

The whispers laughed, cruel and mocking. "You're fooling yourself. He'll leave, just like everyone else."

Mary clenched her fists, her nails digging into her palms. She couldn't let that happen. She had to protect her children, no matter the cost.

The following evening, Mary sat across from Thomas at the same small café where they had shared coffee a week earlier. She had hesitated before accepting his invitation, her fear and paranoia warring with her longing for connection. But now that she was here, she found herself relaxing, if only slightly.

Thomas stirred his coffee absently, his eyes warm as he watched her. "You seem tense," he said gently. "Is everything okay?"

Mary hesitated, unsure how much to reveal. "It's just… hard sometimes," she admitted, her voice barely above a whisper. "Being a single mum. Taking care of everything on my own."

Thomas nodded, his expression sympathetic. "I can't imagine how tough that must be," he said. "But you're doing an amazing job, Mary. It's clear how much you love your kids."

The sincerity in his voice brought tears to Mary's eyes, and she looked away, embarrassed. "Thank you," she said softly. "That means a lot."

They sat in silence for a moment, the noise of the café swirling around them. Mary felt a strange sense of comfort in

Thomas's presence, as though he were a lifeline in a storm she couldn't escape.

"Have you ever thought about getting help?" he asked gently. "You don't have to do this alone."

The question caught Mary off guard, and her chest tightened with a mix of fear and anger. "I don't need help," she said quickly, her voice sharper than she intended. "I can take care of my children."

Thomas held up his hands in a gesture of peace. "I didn't mean to offend you," he said. "I just... want you to know I'm here if you ever need someone to talk to."

Mary's shoulders relaxed slightly, but her guard remained up. The whispers in her mind stirred, their voices warning her to be cautious. She nodded stiffly, offering a faint smile that didn't reach her eyes. "Thank you," she said. "That's kind of you."

That night, as Mary sat in the children's room, her thoughts churned with doubt and confusion. She wanted to believe that Thomas's intentions were pure, that he genuinely cared. But the fear of losing her children, of having her carefully constructed world shattered, was too great to ignore.

She leaned over Emily's bed, brushing her fingers against the stuffed bear. "I won't let anything happen to you," she whispered, her voice trembling. "I'll protect you. No matter what."

The room was silent, but Mary could feel the weight of her children's presence, their love and trust grounding her. She closed her eyes, her tears soaking into the bear's fabric.

"I'll keep you safe," she said, her voice barely audible. "Even if it means losing everything else."

As the night deepened, the whispers returned, their voices soft and insistent. "Protect them," they said. "No one else matters."

Mary nodded to herself, her resolve hardening. She wouldn't let anyone take her children away. Not Thomas. Not the world. No one.

Chapter 14
The Third Victim

The whispers had been relentless all morning, clawing at Mary's mind with venomous accusations. They taunted her, filling her thoughts with images of failure, of people laughing at her, judging her, and plotting to destroy everything she'd worked so hard to protect.

"They're coming for them," one hissed, low and cruel.

"They'll take your children away," another added, its tone sharp and insidious.

Mary gripped the edge of the kitchen counter, her knuckles white as she tried to block out the voices. The sunlight streaming through the window seemed too bright, too harsh, illuminating the cracks in her carefully constructed world. She had spent hours cleaning that morning, scrubbing every surface until her hands were raw, but it still didn't feel like enough.

Her gaze shifted to the children's plates on the table, untouched as usual. She had made them oatmeal with a drizzle of honey, just the way they liked it, but the sight of the uneaten food sent a pang of frustration through her chest.

"Ungrateful," the whispers sneered. "You do everything for them, and they give you nothing in return."

Mary shook her head violently, her nails digging into the counter. "That's not true," she muttered, her voice trembling. "They love me. They need me."

"Do they?" the whispers asked, their tone mocking. "Or are you just fooling yourself?"

The doubt gnawed at her, sharp and unrelenting. She couldn't let the whispers win. She had to stay strong—for Emily and Daniel. They were counting on her.

By the time afternoon rolled around, Mary's nerves were frayed. She decided to go for a walk, hoping the fresh air would clear her mind. She told herself it was for the children's sake; they needed her to be calm, focused, in control. She locked the door behind her, glancing back at the house as though to reassure herself that it would still be there when she returned.

Her footsteps were brisk as she made her way through the neighbourhood, her eyes scanning the familiar streets. The whispers had quieted slightly, their voices now a dull murmur in the back of her mind. But the unease lingered, a constant weight pressing down on her chest.

As she approached the small park at the end of the street, Mary's gaze landed on a group of women gathered near the playground. They stood in a loose circle, their laughter carrying on the breeze as they chatted and sipped coffee. Mary's stomach twisted at the sight of them. They reminded her too much of Jemma—too perfect, too happy, too unaware of the pain that lurked just beneath the surface of the world.

Her eyes narrowed as she focused on one woman in particular. She was tall and slim, with golden hair that fell in loose waves over her shoulders. She wore a bright floral dress that swayed in the breeze, her smile wide and effortless as she spoke to the others. She exuded confidence and warmth, the kind of presence that drew people to her without her even trying.

Mary's chest tightened as a familiar wave of jealousy washed over her. This woman had everything Mary didn't—everything Mary had lost. A perfect life. A perfect family. The kind of happiness that seemed unattainable, no matter how hard Mary tried.

"She's just like the rest of them," the whispers said, their voices dripping with venom. "She doesn't deserve it."

Mary's hands curled into fists at her sides as she stood there, watching. The woman laughed at something one of the others said, the sound light and musical. It grated against Mary's ears, setting her teeth on edge.

"She doesn't know what it's like to lose everything," the whispers continued. "To be left with nothing. She's never suffered the way you have."

The anger simmering beneath Mary's skin began to bubble to the surface, her breathing growing shallow and uneven. She didn't know the woman's name, didn't know anything about her, but that didn't matter. What mattered was the way she stood there, so blissfully unaware of the pain that defined Mary's existence.

"She needs to understand," the whispers urged. "Make her understand."

Mary's feet moved before she realised what she was doing, carrying her toward the playground. Her vision tunnelled, the world around her fading into a blur of colours and sounds. The whispers grew louder, their voices blending into a single, insistent command: *Do it.*

The woman didn't notice Mary at first, too engrossed in her conversation to pay attention to the figure approaching from behind. Mary's steps were silent, her body rigid with tension as she closed the distance between them. Her hand slipped into her coat pocket, her fingers wrapping around the knife she had started carrying with her everywhere she went.

The weight of it was both comforting and terrifying.

"Excuse me," Mary said, her voice steady despite the storm raging inside her.

The woman turned, her bright blue eyes meeting Mary's. Her smile faltered slightly, replaced by a look of polite curiosity. "Yes? Can I help you?"

Mary forced a smile, though it felt foreign on her face. "I just wanted to say... you have a beautiful family."

The woman's expression softened, and she tilted her head slightly. "Oh, thank you," she said, her voice warm. "That's very kind of you to say."

Mary's grip on the knife tightened. "It must be nice," she said, her tone turning bitter despite her efforts to keep it neutral. "To have everything."

The woman's brow furrowed, and she took a small step back, her body tensing. "I'm sorry," she said cautiously. "Do I know you?"

"No," Mary said flatly. "But I know you."

Before the woman could respond, Mary's hand shot out, the knife flashing in the sunlight. The blade found its mark, slashing across the woman's throat with brutal efficiency. Her eyes widened in shock, her hands flying to her neck as blood poured through her fingers.

The playground erupted into chaos. The other women screamed, their coffee cups clattering to the ground as they scrambled away. Children cried, their voices piercing the air as they ran toward their mothers.

Mary stood frozen for a moment, her chest heaving as she stared at the woman crumpled on the ground. Blood pooled around her, soaking into the bright floral fabric of her dress. The whispers in Mary's mind were silent now, their absence almost deafening.

"You'll never be like her," they said finally, their voices faint but cruel. "No matter what you do."

Mary fled the scene, her heart pounding as she weaved through the neighbourhood. She didn't stop until she reached her house, slamming the door shut behind her and locking it with trembling hands. Her chest heaved as she leaned against the door, her mind racing with a mixture of fear and exhilaration.

The children's room was her first destination. She stumbled up the stairs, her legs shaky beneath her, and burst through the door. The sight of the neatly made beds, the stuffed bear perched on Emily's pillow, brought a wave of relief crashing over her.

"I'm home," she whispered, her voice shaking. "Mummy's home."

She sank onto the edge of Daniel's bed, her hands still slick with blood. The adrenaline began to fade, leaving her body heavy and her mind clouded. She clutched the bear to her chest, tears streaming down her face.

"I did it for you," she said, her voice barely audible. "Everything I do is for you."

The room remained silent, but Mary didn't feel alone. Not here. Not with her children.

Chapter 15
The Weight of Suspicion

The neighbourhood was abuzz with news of the murder. Mary could feel it in the way people lingered on their front porches, their voices hushed and cautious as they exchanged worried glances. She had seen the police cars earlier that morning, parked near the playground where the attack had occurred. The flashing lights and yellow tape had drawn a crowd, and though Mary had stayed inside, peeking through the curtains, she could feel the weight of their collective fear.

"They're talking about you," the whispers hissed, their voices sharp and insistent. "They know what you did."

Mary clenched her fists, her nails digging into her palms as she paced the living room. "They don't know anything," she muttered under her breath. "They can't."

But the whispers wouldn't be silenced. They filled her mind with images of neighbours pointing at her house, of police officers knocking on her door, of her children being torn away from her. The thought sent a wave of panic crashing over her, and she sank onto the couch, her chest heaving as she tried to catch her breath.

The television was on, but Mary wasn't paying attention to the images flickering across the screen. Her focus was on the news ticker scrolling along the bottom, the words blurring together as her mind raced.

"Local Woman Killed in Broad Daylight at Neighbourhood Park."

Her stomach churned as she read the words, the weight of her actions pressing down on her like a physical force. She hadn't meant for it to happen—not exactly. The whispers had pushed her, filling her mind with anger and jealousy until she couldn't think clearly. But now that it was done, there was no taking it back.

"You did what you had to do," the whispers said, their tone soothing now. "She deserved it."

Mary shook her head, her tears blurring her vision. "I didn't want to," she whispered, her voice trembling. "I just… I couldn't stop."

"You're protecting them," the whispers reminded her. "You're a good mother."

The words brought a faint sense of comfort, but it was fleeting. Deep down, Mary knew the truth: she was losing control. The world she had built for herself, the life she had tried so hard to protect, was crumbling around her.

Later that day, Mary forced herself to leave the house, if only to keep up appearances. She couldn't afford to draw attention to herself, not now. She grabbed her coat and stepped outside, the cool autumn air biting at her skin. The street was unusually quiet, the tension in the neighbourhood palpable.

As she walked toward the grocery store, Mary kept her head down, avoiding eye contact with the few people she passed. She could feel their eyes on her, their stares burning into her back like a brand. Every step she took felt heavier than the last, the weight of suspicion pressing down on her.

When she reached the store, the familiar hum of fluorescent lights and the murmur of shoppers brought a brief sense of normalcy. Mary grabbed a cart and made her way down the aisles, her movements mechanical as she picked up the items on her list. Milk. Bread. Canned soup. She moved quickly, her mind racing with thoughts she couldn't quiet.

As she turned into the produce section, her heart skipped a beat. Thomas Greene stood near the apples, inspecting each one carefully before placing it in a plastic bag. He hadn't seen her yet, but the sight of him brought a mixture of relief and dread crashing over her.

"Act normal," the whispers urged. "He can't know."

Mary forced herself to take a deep breath before approaching him, her hands gripping the cart tightly to steady herself. "Thomas," she said, her voice wavering slightly.

He looked up, his face lighting up with a warm smile. "Mary! Fancy seeing you here."

Her heart raced as she returned his smile, though it felt forced. "It's good to see you," she said. "How have you been?"

"Not bad," Thomas replied, dropping the last apple into the bag and tying it off. "Though I have to admit, the news lately has been pretty unsettling."

Mary's chest tightened, her smile faltering. "The news?"

Thomas nodded, his expression growing serious. "That poor woman at the park. It's hard to believe something like that could happen so close to home."

Mary swallowed hard, her grip on the cart tightening. "It's terrible," she said, her voice barely above a whisper.

Thomas studied her for a moment, his gaze softening. "You look a little shaken," he said gently. "Are you okay?"

"I'm fine," Mary said quickly, her voice sharper than she intended. She glanced away, her hands trembling as she pretended to adjust the items in her cart. "It's just... a lot to process."

"I get that," Thomas said, his tone kind. "If you ever need someone to talk to, I'm here."

Mary forced herself to meet his gaze, her chest aching with a mix of gratitude and guilt. "Thank you," she said softly. "That means a lot."

Thomas smiled again, his warmth cutting through the tension in her chest. "Anytime, Mary. Don't hesitate to reach out."

The encounter left Mary feeling unsteady, her emotions swirling as she made her way home. She wanted to believe that Thomas cared, that he genuinely wanted to help. But the whispers in her mind were quick to remind her of the danger.

"He'll betray you," they said. "He'll take them away."

Mary shook her head, her hands gripping the steering wheel tightly as she pulled into her driveway. "He wouldn't do that," she muttered. "He's different."

"Are you sure?" the whispers taunted. "You can't trust anyone."

The doubt lingered as Mary stepped into the house, the familiar silence wrapping around her like a suffocating blanket. She locked the door behind her and leaned against it, her body trembling as she tried to steady her breathing.

The children's room was her sanctuary, the only place where she felt truly safe. She climbed the stairs slowly, her legs heavy with exhaustion, and pushed the door open. The sight of the neatly made beds and the soft glow of the nightlight brought a faint sense of relief, but it wasn't enough to quiet her racing thoughts.

Mary sat on the edge of Emily's bed, the stuffed bear clutched tightly to her chest. "I don't know what to do," she whispered, her tears soaking into the bear's fabric. "I'm trying so hard, but it's never enough."

The room remained silent, but Mary felt the weight of her children's presence, their love grounding her in a way nothing else could. She closed her eyes, her breathing slowing as she pressed her forehead against the bear.

"I'll protect you," she said, her voice trembling but resolute. "No matter what it takes."

The whispers grew quieter, their voices fading into the background as Mary's resolve hardened. She couldn't let anyone take her children away. Not the neighbours. Not the police. Not even Thomas.

As the night deepened, Mary sat in the darkened room, her mind churning with plans and possibilities. She didn't know how much longer she could keep this up, but one thing was certain: she would do whatever it took to protect her family.

Chapter 16
Crumbling Facades

Mary woke to the sound of rain tapping against the window. The room was dim, the grey light of the overcast sky casting long shadows across the walls. For a brief moment, she felt the comforting pull of sleep, the weightlessness that came with forgetting. But then the memories came rushing back—the park, the blood, the looks of fear from the other mothers as they screamed and scattered.

Her chest tightened as she sat up, her breath coming in shallow gasps. She pressed her hands against her temples, willing the memories away, but they clung to her like a second skin.

"They're closing in," the whispers said, their voices low and insidious. "It's only a matter of time."

"No," Mary whispered, shaking her head. "They don't know. They can't."

But the doubt lingered, gnawing at the edges of her mind. She glanced toward the children's room, her heart aching as she thought of Emily and Daniel. She couldn't lose them. Not now. Not ever.

The day stretched on in a haze of monotony and unease. Mary moved through her routine with mechanical precision, scrubbing the kitchen counters until her hands ached and vacuuming the living room rug for the third time that week. The whispers followed her everywhere, their voices blending into the background noise of her thoughts.

"You're slipping," they said. "They'll see right through you."

Mary's hands trembled as she wiped down the kitchen table, her mind racing. She couldn't afford to make a mistake. Not now, when everything was so precariously balanced. She had to keep up appearances, to convince everyone—including herself—that everything was fine.

But the strain was taking its toll. Her reflection in the window looked like a stranger's—her eyes hollow, her face pale and drawn. The weight of the murders, the lies, and the ever-present threat of exposure was crushing her, piece by piece.

That afternoon, Mary decided to go for a walk. She needed air, space to think. The rain had stopped, leaving the streets damp and glistening under the weak sunlight. She locked the door behind her, glancing back at the house to reassure herself that it would be safe while she was gone.

Her footsteps echoed softly as she made her way down the street, her head down and her coat pulled tight around her. She avoided eye contact with the neighbours, her chest tightening whenever she passed a house with curtains drawn back. She could feel their eyes on her, their stares burning into her back.

"They're talking about you," the whispers said. "They know what you've done."

Mary clenched her fists, her nails digging into her palms. "They don't know anything," she muttered under her breath. "They're just paranoid."

But even as she said the words, the doubt lingered. She turned the corner, her thoughts churning, and nearly walked straight into Thomas Greene.

Mary!" Thomas said, his voice filled with surprise. "Are you all right?"

Mary stumbled back a step, her heart pounding. She forced a smile, though it felt brittle and insincere. "Thomas," she said, her voice shaky. "I didn't see you there."

Thomas studied her closely, his brow furrowing. "You look… off," he said gently. "Is everything okay?"

Mary hesitated, her mind racing. She wanted to tell him the truth, to unburden herself of the weight that was crushing her. But the whispers were quick to intervene.

"Don't trust him," they warned. "He'll betray you."

"I'm fine," Mary said quickly, her voice sharper than she intended. She averted her gaze, her hands gripping the edges of her coat. "Just… tired, that's all."

Thomas didn't look convinced, but he nodded slowly. "If you say so," he said. "But you know you can talk to me, right? About anything."

The sincerity in his voice brought a lump to Mary's throat, and she looked away, blinking back tears. "Thank you," she said softly. "That means a lot."

They walked together for a while, the conversation light and easy. Thomas told her about his work as a theatre support worker, his sister, and his plans to visit his family for the holidays. Mary listened, her tension easing slightly with each passing moment. There was something comforting about his presence, something that made her feel almost normal.

But the whispers wouldn't let her forget. They lingered at the edges of her mind, their voices growing louder with each step.

"He's dangerous," they said. "He'll ruin everything."

Mary's chest tightened, and she stopped walking, her hands clenching into fists at her sides. "I should go," she said abruptly, her voice trembling. "The children are waiting for me."

Thomas frowned, concern flickering across his face. "Are you sure? You look like you could use some company."

"I'm sure," Mary said quickly, avoiding his gaze. "Thank you, though."

Before Thomas could respond, Mary turned and walked away, her footsteps hurried and uneven. The whispers followed her, their voices triumphant.

"See?" they said. "He can't be trusted."

By the time Mary reached her house, her nerves were frayed. She locked the door behind her, her hands shaking as she turned the deadbolt. The house was silent, the faint hum of the refrigerator the only sound. Mary leaned against the door, her chest heaving as she tried to steady her breathing.

She climbed the stairs to the children's room, her heart aching as she stepped inside. The sight of the neatly made beds and the stuffed bear on Emily's pillow brought a faint sense of comfort, but it wasn't enough to quiet her racing thoughts.

"I'm home," she said softly, her voice trembling. "Mummy's here."

She sat on the edge of Daniel's bed, clutching the stuffed bear to her chest. Her tears soaked into the fabric as she whispered to the empty room.

"I'm trying so hard," she said, her voice breaking. "But it's never enough."

The whispers grew quieter, their voices fading into the background. But their presence remained, a constant reminder of the darkness that had taken root inside her.

The next morning, Mary woke to the sound of knocking. Her heart raced as she sat up, her mind immediately jumping to the worst-case scenario. The police. The neighbours. Thomas.

She made her way to the front door, her hands trembling as she unlocked it. To her surprise, it was Mrs. Turner, her nosy neighbour from across the street. The woman stood on the porch, her arms crossed and her expression stern.

"Good morning, Mary," she said, her tone clipped. "I wanted to talk to you about something."

Mary's chest tightened as she forced a smile. "Of course," she said, her voice shaky. "What's on your mind?"

Mrs. Turner glanced around as if making sure no one else was listening before leaning in slightly. "There's been talk in the neighbourhood," she said, her voice low. "About the... incident at the park."

Mary's heart skipped a beat, but she kept her expression neutral. "Oh?"

"People are worried," Mrs. Turner continued, her eyes narrowing slightly. "There's been some... speculation about who might be responsible."

Mary's hands clenched at her sides, her mind racing. "Do they have any suspects?" she asked, her voice steady despite the panic bubbling beneath the surface.

Mrs. Turner hesitated, her gaze sharp. "Not yet," she said. "But people are watching, Mary. Everyone's on edge."

The words hung in the air, heavy with implication. Mary forced another smile, though her heart was pounding. "Thank you for letting me know," she said. "I'll be careful."

Mrs. Turner nodded, her eyes lingering on Mary for a moment before she turned and walked away. Mary closed the door, her body trembling as she leaned against it.

"They know," the whispers said, their voices dripping with malice. "It's only a matter of time."

Mary clenched her fists, her nails digging into her palms again. "No," she whispered. "They don't. They can't."

But the doubt lingered, gnawing at her like a cancer. She couldn't afford to make another mistake. Not now. Not when everything was so close to falling apart.

Chapter 17
Shadows of Truth

The morning light filtered weakly through the curtains as Mary sat at the kitchen table, her hands wrapped tightly around a steaming mug of tea. She hadn't slept at all the night before. The whispers had kept her awake, filling her mind with warnings and accusations. Even now, as she stared at the untouched breakfast plates set neatly on the table, their voices clawed at her thoughts.

"They're closing in," they hissed. "You're losing control."

Mary shook her head, her grip on the mug tightening. "I'm not," she muttered under her breath. "Everything is fine."

But even as she said the words, doubt lingered. Mrs. Turner's visit the day before had shaken her more than she cared to admit. The woman's sharp gaze, her careful words—there had been something pointed about the interaction, as though Mrs. Turner had been probing for cracks in Mary's facade.

"She knows," the whispers taunted. "She's watching you."

Mary pushed the mug away, her appetite gone. She couldn't sit here. She needed to move, to do something—

anything—to quiet the storm in her mind. She stood abruptly, grabbing the plates from the table and dumping their contents into the trash.

"Ungrateful," she muttered as she rinsed the plates under the tap. "You don't even bother to come down."

The silence of the house was deafening, pressing against her like a weight. Mary dried her hands and glanced toward the staircase, her chest tightening. She needed to check on them to make sure they were safe.

The children's room was exactly as she had left it the night before. Emily's pink quilt was perfectly smoothed, the stuffed bear sitting upright on the pillow. Daniel's blue comforter was neatly tucked, the desk in the corner organised down to the smallest detail.

Mary stood in the doorway, her hands clenched at her sides as she surveyed the room. Everything was in its place. Everything was as it should be.

"I'm doing this for you," she said softly, her voice trembling. "Everything I do is for you."

She moved to Emily's bed, sitting on the edge and picking up the bear. Its fur was worn, its button eyes slightly loose, but it brought her a faint sense of comfort. She clutched it to her chest, closing her eyes as tears slipped down her cheeks.

"You're all I have," she whispered. "I won't let anyone take you away."

The whispers grew quieter, their voices fading into the background. For a moment, Mary allowed herself to believe that she was safe, that her children were safe. But the moment was fleeting, and the doubt returned like a tide, pulling her under.

Later that day, Mary found herself at the grocery store again, wandering the aisles with no real purpose. The fluorescent lights buzzed faintly overhead, and the hum of conversation around her felt distant, almost unreal. She pushed her cart aimlessly, her thoughts churning.

When she turned into the coffee aisle, she nearly collided with Thomas Greene. He looked up, startled at first, but then his expression softened into a smile.

"Mary," he said warmly. "We have to stop meeting like this."

Mary managed a weak smile, though her heart was racing. "Thomas," she said, her voice quieter than she intended. "Hello."

He studied her closely, his brow furrowing slightly. "You look tired," he said gently. "Is everything okay?"

Mary hesitated, unsure of how to respond. Part of her wanted to tell him the truth, to unburden herself of the weight she carried. But the whispers were quick to intervene.

"Don't trust him," they said. "He'll destroy everything."

"I'm fine," Mary said quickly, her voice sharper than she intended. She forced a smile, though it felt brittle. "Just… a lot on my mind."

Thomas nodded slowly, his concern evident. "Well, if you ever want to talk, I'm here," he said. "I mean that."

The sincerity in his voice brought a lump to Mary's throat, and she looked away, blinking back tears. "Thank you," she said softly. "That means a lot."

That evening, Mary sat in the children's room, the stuffed bear clutched tightly in her hands. The house was silent, save for the faint hum of the refrigerator and the occasional creak of the floorboards. She stared at the neatly made beds, her chest aching with a mix of love and desperation.

"I met someone," she said softly, her voice trembling. "His name is Thomas. I think... I think you'd like him."

The words felt strange, foreign, as though they belonged to someone else. Mary closed her eyes, her tears soaking into the bear's worn fur. "He's kind," she continued. "He makes me feel... less alone."

The room remained silent, but Mary imagined she could feel her children's presence, their love and trust wrapping around her like a blanket. She clung to that feeling, letting it anchor her.

But the whispers were never far away.

"He'll take them from you," they warned. "He'll ruin everything."

Mary's hands trembled as she gripped the bear tighter. "No," she whispered. "He wouldn't do that."

"Are you sure?" the whispers taunted. "You can't trust anyone."

The doubt gnawed at her, sharp and unrelenting. She wanted to believe in Thomas, in the possibility of a future where she wasn't alone. But the fear of losing her children, of having her carefully constructed world torn apart, was too great to ignore.

"I won't let that happen," she said aloud, her voice firm. "I'll protect them. No matter what."

The next day, Mary received a call from Thomas. His voice was warm and friendly, but there was an edge of hesitation that set her on edge.

"I was wondering if you'd like to grab coffee again," he said. "Just to talk. No pressure."

Mary hesitated, her mind racing. She wanted to say yes, to accept the kindness he offered so freely. But the whispers were quick to remind her of the danger.

"You can't let him in," they said. "He'll see the cracks."

"I'm not sure," Mary said finally, her voice shaky. "I have a lot going on right now."

Thomas didn't press her, but she could hear the disappointment in his voice. "I understand," he said. "Just... know that I'm here if you need me."

Mary ended the call, her chest tightening as she placed the phone back on the counter. She felt torn, caught between her desire for connection and her fear of vulnerability. The walls of her world were closing in, and she didn't know how much longer she could hold them up.

That night, Mary sat in the darkened living room, her thoughts churning. The whispers were louder than ever, their voices blending into a cacophony of fear and doubt. She pressed her hands against her ears, but it did nothing to drown them out.

"You're losing control," they said. "They'll take everything from you."

Mary's chest heaved as she struggled to breathe. She felt like she was drowning, the weight of her secrets dragging her under. She wanted to scream, to lash out, to make the voices stop.

But she couldn't. Not yet. Not while her children still needed her.

"I'll keep them safe," she whispered, her voice trembling. "I'll do whatever it takes."

The whispers grew quieter, their voices fading into the background. But their presence remained, a constant reminder of the darkness that had taken root inside her.

Chapter 18
A Breach of Trust

The sky hung heavy with the promise of rain as Mary stared out the window, her fingers curling tightly around the edge of the curtain. The whispers were particularly loud today, their accusations slicing through her thoughts with relentless precision.

"He's watching you," they hissed.

"He's waiting for you to slip."

Mary's jaw tightened as her gaze darted toward Thomas's house, a few streets away. She had never asked exactly where he lived, but she had pieced it together from little clues during their conversations. He had mentioned a house with blue shutters, a small garden out front, and a single oak tree shading the driveway. She'd driven past it once, just to confirm, her chest tight with a mix of curiosity and unease.

The whispers had begun to focus on Thomas after that drive. They had latched onto her doubts, magnifying them until they felt undeniable.

"You let him in too far," they said. "He's dangerous."

Mary stepped back from the window, her stomach churning. She didn't want to believe it, didn't want to think that Thomas—kind, understanding Thomas—could be a threat. But the whispers had never been wrong before. They knew things she didn't. They saw dangers she couldn't.

"He'll destroy everything," they warned. "You have to stop him."

Mary spent the morning cleaning the house, her movements sharp and mechanical. She scrubbed the counters until her hands ached, vacuumed the carpets twice, and wiped down the windows, even though they didn't need it. The repetitive tasks gave her something to focus on, a way to drown out the noise in her mind.

But no matter how hard she worked, the whispers persisted, their voices growing louder with each passing hour.

"He's too close to the truth," they said. "He'll take them from you."

Mary paused, her grip tightening on the rag she had been using to clean the kitchen table. The thought of losing Emily and Daniel made her chest ache, her breath catching in her throat. She had worked so hard to protect them, to keep them safe from the cruel, unforgiving world outside these walls. She couldn't let anyone take that away from her.

Not even Thomas.

By midday, Mary's anxiety had reached a breaking point. She couldn't stay in the house any longer, couldn't bear the oppressive silence pressing down on her. She grabbed her coat and keys, locking the door behind her as she stepped into the cool, damp air.

Her feet carried her toward Thomas's house almost unconsciously. She didn't have a plan, didn't know what she intended to do when she got there. All she knew was that the whispers wouldn't stop until she confronted the source of her unease.

The blue shutters came into view as Mary turned the corner, her heart pounding in her chest. The small garden in front of the house was neatly tended, the flowers bright and cheerful despite the grey sky overhead. The oak tree's branches swayed gently in the breeze, their leaves whispering secrets of their own.

Mary slowed her pace, her hands trembling as she approached the driveway. She felt exposed, vulnerable, as though the house itself was watching her. She scanned the windows for any sign of movement, her breath catching when she spotted Thomas sitting at the dining table, his back to her.

"He's hiding something," the whispers said. "Find out what it is."

Mary's gaze shifted to the mailbox near the curb. It was slightly ajar, a stack of letters visible inside. Her heart raced as an idea took hold, the whispers urging her forward.

"Check the mail," they said. "He won't know."

Mary glanced around, her eyes darting to the empty street. No one was watching. No one would see. She hesitated for only a moment before stepping toward the mailbox, her fingers trembling as she pulled it open.

The letters were ordinary at first glance—bills, advertisements, a magazine subscription. But as Mary flipped through them, one caught her attention. The return address was from the local police department, the bold lettering stark against the plain white envelope.

Her stomach dropped as she stared at the envelope, her mind racing. Why would Thomas be receiving mail from the police? Was he involved in the investigation? Had he been watching her, gathering evidence, waiting for the right moment to strike?

"You were right," the whispers said, their tone triumphant. "He's dangerous."

Mary shoved the letters back into the mailbox, her breath coming in short, panicked gasps. She turned and walked quickly back to the sidewalk, her mind a whirlwind of fear and anger. The betrayal felt like a physical blow, sharp and unrelenting.

She had trusted him. She had let him get close, let him see parts of her life she had kept hidden from everyone else. And now he was going to use it against her, to tear apart everything she had worked so hard to protect.

Mary spent the rest of the day pacing the house, her thoughts spiralling further into darkness. The whispers fed her paranoia, their voices growing louder and more insistent.

"You have to stop him," they said. "Before he destroys you."

Her hands shook as she clutched Emily's stuffed bear, the worn fabric soft against her palms. She sat on the edge of the bed, her tears soaking into the bear's fur as she whispered to the empty room.

"I won't let him hurt you," she said, her voice trembling. "I'll keep you safe. I promise."

The room remained silent, but Mary could feel the weight of her children's presence, their love grounding her in a way nothing else could. She clung to that feeling, letting it anchor her as the storm inside her raged on.

That evening, Mary received a text from Thomas. The sight of his name on her phone made her stomach turn, her hands shaking as she opened the message.

Thomas: Hey, just checking in. Haven't heard from you. Hope you're doing okay.

Mary stared at the words, her chest tightening. She wanted to believe that his concern was genuine, that he cared about her in the way he claimed. But the envelope from the police department loomed large in her mind, a constant reminder of his potential betrayal.

"He's lying," the whispers said. "He's just trying to get close enough to strike."

Mary's fingers hovered over the keyboard as she debated how to respond. Part of her wanted to confront him, to demand answers. But another part of her—the part that listened to the whispers—knew she couldn't afford to tip her hand.

Mary: I'm fine. Just busy. Thanks for checking in.

She hit send, her hands trembling as she set the phone down. The simple act of responding felt exhausting, the weight of her paranoia pressing down on her like a physical force.

The next day, Mary's resolve hardened. She couldn't sit back and wait for Thomas to make his move. She had to act first, to protect herself and her children before it was too late.

She spent the morning preparing, her movements calm and deliberate. She cleaned the house from top to bottom, ensuring that everything was in its place. She set the children's plates on the table, arranging them with meticulous care. And when everything was ready, she stood in the middle of the living room, her hands clenched into fists at her sides.

"I'm doing this for you," she said softly, her voice trembling. "Everything I do is for you."

The whispers were silent, their presence fading into the background. For the first time in days, Mary felt a sense of clarity, a calm certainty about what she needed to do.

As the rain began to fall outside, Mary grabbed her coat and stepped into the cool, damp air. The path ahead was clear, the whispers her only guide. She would protect her children at any cost, even if it meant confronting Thomas and uncovering the truth.

Chapter 19
A Fragile Confrontation

The rain fell steadily as Mary walked down the street, her coat pulled tightly around her to ward off the chill. The whispers in her mind had grown quieter, but their presence still lingered, a constant undercurrent to her thoughts.

"He knows too much," they said softly, almost soothingly. "You can't let him get closer."

Mary's jaw tightened as she approached Thomas's house. The blue shutters looked dull under the grey sky; the small garden out front battered by the rain. She stopped at the edge of the driveway, her heart pounding in her chest.

She didn't know what she was going to say. Part of her wanted to confront him, to demand an explanation for the letter from the police department. But another part of her—the part ruled by fear and suspicion—knew that she couldn't trust anything he said.

"Stay in control," the whispers urged. "Don't let him see your fear."

Mary took a deep breath, her hands trembling as she climbed the steps to the front door. She hesitated for a moment, her mind racing, before raising her hand and knocking firmly.

The door opened after a few moments, revealing Thomas standing there, a look of mild surprise on his face. He was dressed casually, his hair slightly damps from the rain, and his expression softened when he saw her.

"Mary," he said warmly. "I wasn't expecting you. Come in out of the rain."

Mary stepped inside without a word, the warmth of the house enveloping her as Thomas closed the door behind her. She stood in the entryway, her coat dripping onto the floor, as she glanced around. The interior of the house was cosy and inviting, with soft lighting and neatly arranged furniture. It was a stark contrast to the chaos swirling inside her mind.

"Is everything okay?" Thomas asked, his tone gentle. "You look… upset."

Mary turned to face him; her hands clenched into fists at her sides. "I found something," she said, her voice trembling. "Something I need you to explain."

Thomas frowned, his brow furrowing in confusion. "What are you talking about?"

Mary reached into her pocket and pulled out the envelope she had taken from his mailbox, her fingers shaking as she held it up. "This," she said sharply. "Why are you getting letters from the police?"

Thomas's eyes widened as he looked at the envelope, his confusion deepening. "Mary, where did you get that?"

"It doesn't matter," she snapped, her voice rising. "What matters is what it means. Are you working with them? Are you trying to take my children away?"

Thomas took a step back, his hands raised in a gesture of peace. "Mary, slow down," he said calmly. "I'm not working with anyone. I have no idea what you're talking about."

"Don't lie to me!" Mary shouted, her chest heaving. "I trusted you, and now I find this? How do you expect me to believe you?"

Thomas's expression shifted; concern etched into his features. "Mary," he said softly, his tone careful. "You've been under a lot of stress. I think maybe you're misinterpreting things."

Mary's breath caught in her throat, her mind racing. His calm demeanour only fuelled her suspicions, the whispers in her mind growing louder.

"He's trying to manipulate you," they said. "Don't fall for it."

"I'm not crazy," Mary said through clenched teeth, her voice trembling. "I know what I saw."

Thomas took another step back, his gaze steady but wary. "I'm not saying you're crazy," he said carefully. "I'm saying that maybe… maybe you need someone to talk to. Someone who can help."

The words hit Mary like a slap, her chest tightening as anger and fear surged within her. "You think I need help?" she spat. "You think I'm the problem?"

"Mary, please," Thomas said, his voice pleading. "I just want to help you."

The sincerity in his voice brought tears to Mary's eyes, but it also made her angrier. She couldn't trust him. Not now. Not ever.

"You don't care about me," she said bitterly. "You just want to take my children away."

Thomas's eyes widened, a flicker of confusion crossing his face. "Mary… what children?"

The room seemed to tilt, the air growing heavy around her. Mary's chest heaved as she stared at him, her mind struggling to process his words.

"What do you mean, 'what children?'" she demanded, her voice shaking. "Emily and Daniel. My children."

Thomas hesitated, his expression pained. "Mary," he said gently. "There are no children. I've been to your house. I've never seen them."

Mary stumbled back, her hand clutching the back of a chair for support. "You're lying," she said, her voice breaking. "You're trying to confuse me."

"I'm not lying," Thomas said firmly. "Mary, please listen to me. I don't know what's going on, but I want to help you. You're not alone in this."

The room spun around her, her vision blurring as the weight of his words settled over her. No children. The thought was unthinkable, impossible. She had held them, fed them, cared for them. They were real. They had to be.

"They're real," she whispered, her voice trembling. "They're real."

Thomas stepped closer, his movements cautious. "Mary," he said softly. "I think you've been through something traumatic. Maybe your mind—"

"No!" Mary screamed, cutting him off. "You don't understand! You don't know what I've been through!"

Thomas stopped, his hands raised in a gesture of surrender. "You're right," he said gently. "I don't. But I want to understand. I want to help."

Mary's hands shook as she clutched the chair, her tears streaming down her face. The whispers in her mind were deafening now, their voices a cacophony of fear and anger.

"Don't trust him," they said. "He'll destroy everything."

"I can't," Mary sobbed, her voice barely audible. "I can't do this."

Thomas stepped closer, his voice soft and steady. "You're stronger than you think," he said. "But you don't have to do it alone."

Mary looked up at him, her vision blurred by tears. For a moment, she saw something in his eyes—kindness, understanding, maybe even love. But the fear and doubt were too strong, the whispers too loud.

Without thinking, Mary grabbed the letter from the table and shoved it into her pocket. She turned and fled, the sound of Thomas calling her name fading as she stumbled out the door and into the rain.

Mary's chest heaved as she ran, her tears mingling with the raindrops on her face. She didn't stop until she reached her house, her hands shaking as she unlocked the door and stepped inside. The silence enveloped her, but it offered no comfort.

She climbed the stairs to the children's room, her breath catching in her throat as she pushed the door open. The sight of the neatly made beds and the stuffed bear on Emily's pillow brought a fresh wave of tears to her eyes.

"They're real," she whispered, her voice trembling. "They're real."

But the doubt lingered, gnawing at the edges of her mind. Thomas's words echoed in her ears, their weight threatening to crush her.

"There are no children."

Mary sank onto the edge of Emily's bed, clutching the bear tightly to her chest. Her tears soaked into the worn fabric as she rocked back and forth, the whispers in her mind growing quieter.

"I'll protect you," she said softly, her voice trembling. "No matter what. I'll protect you."

The room remained silent, but Mary could feel the weight of her children's presence, their love grounding her in a way nothing else could. She clung to that feeling, letting it anchor her as the storm inside her raged on.

Chapter 20
The Breaking Point

The storm outside matched the one raging in Mary's mind. Rain lashed against the windows, and distant thunder rolled through the dark sky. She sat in the children's room, her back pressed against the wall, clutching Emily's stuffed bear as though it were the only thing tethering her to reality. Her breathing was shallow, her eyes darting around the room as if expecting the walls to collapse in on her.

"They're lying to you," the whispers hissed. "Everyone is lying to you."

Mary clenched her jaw, her hands tightening around the bear. "I know," she whispered, her voice trembling. "I won't let them take you away."

Her gaze drifted to the beds—Emily's neatly tucked pink quilt and Daniel's perfectly smoothed blue comforter. The sight brought a small, fleeting sense of calm, but it was quickly overtaken by the weight of doubt. Thomas's words replayed in her mind, cutting through her like a knife.

"There are no children."

"No," Mary said aloud, shaking her head violently. "He's wrong. He doesn't understand."

But the seed of doubt had been planted, and it was growing, its roots winding through her thoughts. She remembered the way people looked at her when she spoke about her children, the confusion and discomfort in their eyes. She remembered the empty plates at the table, the untouched toys on the shelves. The memories felt like fragments of a dream, slipping further from her grasp the harder she tried to hold onto them.

Mary stood abruptly, the bear slipping from her hands and landing on the floor. She couldn't stay in the house. The walls felt too close, the silence too loud. She needed air, needed to think. She grabbed her coat and stumbled down the stairs, her mind racing.

The storm greeted her as she stepped outside, the rain soaking through her clothes almost instantly. She didn't care. She walked down the street with no destination in mind, her arms wrapped tightly around herself. The whispers followed her, their voices a constant presence in the back of her mind.

"You've let them in too far," they said. "You need to take control."

Her steps quickened as she turned onto the main road, her thoughts spiralling. The streetlights cast long, distorted shadows across the wet pavement, and Mary felt as though the entire world were watching her. She could feel their eyes, their judgement.

"They think you're crazy," the whispers said. "Prove them wrong."

Mary's feet carried her to a familiar house—the one with the blue shutters and the oak tree in the front yard. Thomas's house. Her chest tightened as she stared at it, her mind churning with fear and anger. She thought of the letter from the police, of his calm, measured words during their confrontation.

He was lying. He had to be. There was no other explanation.

The lights were on inside, casting a warm glow that contrasted sharply with the cold, stormy night. Mary stepped closer, her heart pounding in her chest. She could see Thomas through the window, sitting at the dining table with a mug of tea in his hands. He looked relaxed, at ease, as though he didn't have a care in the world.

"He's planning something," the whispers said. "He's waiting for the right moment to strike."

Mary's hands shook as she reached into her pocket, her fingers closing around the handle of the knife she had started carrying with her everywhere she went. The weight of it was both comforting and terrifying.

"I have to stop him," she whispered, her voice trembling. "I have to protect them."

Her footsteps were silent as she approached the front door. She hesitated for only a moment before knocking, her knuckles rapping against the wood with a sense of finality. The sound echoed in the night, mingling with the rhythm of the rain.

Thomas opened the door after a moment, his expression shifting from surprise to concern when he saw her. "Mary," he said, his tone soft. "What are you doing here? You're soaked. Come inside."

Mary stepped past him without a word, her movements stiff and deliberate. Thomas closed the door behind her, his brow furrowing as he watched her.

"Are you okay?" he asked carefully. "You seem... upset."

Mary turned to face him, her hand still in her pocket, gripping the knife tightly. "You lied to me," she said, her voice shaking. "You told me there were no children."

Thomas's expression softened, a flicker of sadness crossing his face. "Mary," he said gently. "I didn't mean to hurt you. I just… I think you've been through something, and—"

"Don't," Mary snapped, cutting him off. "Don't try to twist this. Don't try to make me doubt myself."

"I'm not trying to do that," Thomas said, his tone calm but firm. "I care about you. I want to help you."

The sincerity in his voice brought tears to Mary's eyes, but it also fuelled her anger. She couldn't trust him. She couldn't trust anyone.

"You don't understand," she said, her voice breaking. "You don't know what it's like to lose everything."

Thomas took a step closer, his movements slow and cautious. "Then help me understand," he said. "Talk to me, Mary. Tell me what you're feeling."

Mary's grip on the knife tightened as she took a step back, her chest heaving. "You don't care," she said bitterly. "You just want to take them away."

Thomas froze, his eyes widening slightly. "Take who away?" he asked carefully.

"Emily and Daniel," Mary said, her voice trembling. "My children."

Thomas hesitated, his gaze steady but pained. "Mary," he said softly. "They're not real."

The words hit her like a blow, knocking the air from her lungs. For a moment, the room seemed to tilt, the walls closing in around her. She shook her head violently, tears streaming down her face.

"No," she whispered. "You're lying."

"I'm not," Thomas said, his voice gentle but unwavering. "I've been to your house, Mary. I've seen the empty beds, the untouched toys. There's no one there."

Mary's mind raced, her thoughts a chaotic blur. The images of her children—their laughter, their smiles, their presence—felt so real. They *were* real. They had to be.

"They're real," she said, her voice rising. "They're real!"

Thomas took another step closer, his hands raised in a gesture of peace. "Mary," he said softly. "I know this is hard to hear, but you've been through something traumatic. Your mind—"

"Don't!" Mary screamed, pulling the knife from her pocket. The blade glinted in the dim light, and Thomas froze, his eyes widening.

"Mary," he said carefully, his voice steady. "Put the knife down. We can talk about this."

"No!" she shouted, her hands shaking. "You're trying to take them from me! I won't let you!"

Thomas remained still, his expression calm but alert. "I'm not trying to take anything from you," he said. "I just want to help."

The whispers in Mary's mind were deafening now, their voices blending into a single, insistent command: *Protect them.*

She lunged forward, the knife slashing through the air. Thomas moved quickly, grabbing her wrist and twisting it, forcing the blade from her hand. It clattered to the floor as he pushed her back, his grip firm but careful.

Mary stumbled, her breath coming in ragged gasps as she stared at him, her tears blurring her vision. "You don't understand," she sobbed. "They need me."

Thomas's expression softened; his voice steady but filled with emotion. "Mary," he said. "Look around. There's no one here but us. You're not alone, but you need help. Please let me help you."

Mary sank to the floor, her body trembling as the weight of his words pressed down on her. The whispers were silent now, their absence almost deafening. For the first time, she felt the edges of her reality begin to crack.

"I don't know what's real anymore," she whispered, her voice barely audible.

Thomas knelt beside her, his hand resting gently on her shoulder. "We'll figure it out together," he said softly. "You don't have to do this alone."

Mary closed her eyes, her tears falling freely as the storm outside raged on. For the first time in years, she allowed herself to feel the full weight of her pain, her fear, and her doubt. And for the first time, she let someone else share that burden.

Chapter 21
The Children Are Gone

The storm had passed by the time Mary returned home. The streets glistened under the faint light of the moon, and the cool night air carried the scent of rain-soaked earth. She moved mechanically, her feet dragging across the pavement as though the weight of the world had settled on her shoulders. Thomas's words echoed in her mind, each syllable cutting deeper than the last.

"There are no children."

Mary's hands trembled as she unlocked the front door and stepped inside. The house was silent, its emptiness palpable. She stood in the entryway for a moment, her chest heaving as she struggled to catch her breath. Her coat dripped water onto the floor, but she didn't care. The whispers in her mind were gone now, their absence leaving a deafening void.

"They're real," she whispered to herself, her voice trembling. "They're real."

She climbed the stairs slowly, each step feeling heavier than the last. When she reached the children's room, she hesitated, her hand hovering over the doorknob. Her heart pounded in her chest as she finally turned the knob and pushed the door open.

The room was exactly as she had left it. Emily's pink quilt was perfectly smoothed, the stuffed bear sitting upright on her pillow. Daniel's blue comforter was tucked neatly, the desk in the corner still meticulously organised. It was perfect. Too perfect.

Mary stepped inside, her movements slow and deliberate. She moved to Emily's bed first, running her fingers over the quilt. It felt real. Solid. Tangible. She picked up the bear, clutching it to her chest as tears streamed down her face.

"They're here," she said softly, her voice breaking. "I know they're here."

But the room remained silent, its stillness oppressive. Mary's gaze shifted to Daniel's bed, her chest tightening as she took a step toward it. She sank onto the edge, her hands trembling as she smoothed the comforter. It was cold beneath her touch, untouched.

The doubt that had been gnawing at her finally broke through, and the world seemed to tilt around her. She thought of the empty plates at the table, the untouched toys, the way people looked at her when she spoke of her children. She thought of Thomas's words, his pained expression as he tried to make her see the truth.

"There are no children."

Mary dropped the bear onto the floor, her hands flying to her head as she let out a strangled sob. "No!" she screamed, her voice raw with anguish. "They're real! They're real!"

The walls of the room seemed to close in on her, the air growing heavy as her sobs filled the space. She rocked back and forth, her tears soaking into her skirt as she clutched her knees to her chest.

The memories that had once felt so vivid now seemed hazy, like fragments of a dream slipping through her fingers. She remembered holding Emily in her arms, her laughter filling the room. She remembered teaching Daniel how to tie his shoes, his face lighting up with pride when he finally succeeded. But now, those memories felt distant, disconnected from reality.

"What's happening to me?" she whispered, her voice trembling. "Why can't I remember?"

Mary stood abruptly, her movements frantic as she began tearing through the room. She opened the dresser drawers, pulling out clothes and scattering them across the floor. She yanked books from the shelves, their pages fluttering like broken wings. She rummaged through the closet, searching for something—anything—that would prove her children were real.

But the more she searched, the more her desperation grew. The clothes were neatly folded but unworn, their fabric stiff with disuse. The books had no creases in their spines, their pages untouched. The toys in the closet were pristine, their surfaces unmarked by the wear and tear of playful hands.

"No," Mary whispered, shaking her head. "This isn't right. This isn't right."

She collapsed onto the floor, her hands trembling as she picked up one of Daniel's shirts. It felt so real in her hands, but the absence of any sign of him made her chest ache with a hollow pain she couldn't describe.

"They're real," she said again, her voice barely audible. "They have to be."

Hours passed as Mary sat on the floor, surrounded by the remnants of her search. The room was a mess now, the once-perfect beds undone, the dresser emptied, the shelves bare. The stuffed bear lay discarded by the door, its button eyes staring blankly at the ceiling.

Mary's body felt heavy, her mind numb as she stared at the chaos around her. The doubt that had been gnawing at her had grown into certainty, and the weight of it threatened to crush her.

Thomas had been right. There were no children.

The realisation hit her like a tidal wave, pulling her under and leaving her gasping for air. She had built her entire life around Emily and Daniel, around protecting them, caring for them, loving them. Without them, who was she? What was left of her?

"I don't understand," she whispered, her voice breaking. "How could this happen? How could I not know?"

The silence of the room offered no answers, only the faint hum of the nightlight casting soft shadows across the walls. Mary closed her eyes, her tears streaming down her face as the weight of her grief consumed her.

As the first light of dawn began to filter through the curtains, Mary forced herself to stand. Her legs trembled beneath her, her body heavy with exhaustion. She moved slowly, her hands shaking as she began to tidy the room. She smoothed Emily's quilt, set the bear back on her pillow, and tucked Daniel's comforter neatly into place. She folded the clothes she had scattered, stacking them carefully in the dresser. She put the books back on the shelves, aligning them perfectly.

By the time she was done, the room looked just as it had before. Perfect. Peaceful. Deceptive.

Mary stood in the doorway, her hand resting on the frame as she took one last look at the room. It was empty now, its stillness a stark contrast to the chaos in her mind.

"I'm sorry," she whispered, her voice trembling. "I'm so sorry."

Mary made her way downstairs, her movements slow and deliberate. The house felt foreign now, its silence oppressive. She sat at the kitchen table, staring at the empty plates she had set out the night before. The sight of them brought a fresh wave of tears to her eyes, and she covered her face with her hands as her body shook with silent sobs.

For the first time in years, Mary allowed herself to feel the full weight of her loneliness. The whispers that had once comforted her were gone now, their absence leaving a void she didn't know how to fill. She was alone, truly alone, and the pain of that realisation was unbearable.

As the day stretched on, Mary moved through the house in a daze, her mind numb. She cleaned the kitchen, wiped down the counters, and swept the floors, her movements mechanical. She needed to keep busy, to keep moving, to keep the crushing weight of her grief at bay.

But no matter how much she tried to distract herself, the truth lingered, unrelenting. Her children were gone. They had never been there. And now, without them, she didn't know who she was.

As the sun began to set, Mary sat in the living room, staring out the window at the darkening sky. The house was quiet, the silence broken only by the faint ticking of the clock on the wall. She felt hollow, her body heavy with exhaustion but her mind too restless to find peace.

"I can't do this anymore," she whispered, her voice trembling. "I can't."

Mary stood slowly, her legs trembling as she made her way to the stairs. She climbed them one by one, her hand gripping the railing tightly to steady herself. When she reached the top, she turned toward the children's room, her heart aching as she stepped inside.

The room was bathed in the soft glow of the nightlight, its perfect stillness mocking her. She moved to Emily's bed, sitting on the edge and picking up the stuffed bear. She held it tightly to her chest, her tears soaking into its worn fabric.

"I'm so sorry," she whispered, her voice breaking. "I tried so hard. I just… I don't know what to do anymore."

The room remained silent, its emptiness pressing down on her like a weight. Mary closed her eyes, her body trembling as she clung to the bear.

For the first time, she allowed herself to imagine a world without Emily and Daniel. A world where she was alone. A world where she didn't have to fight anymore.

The thought was both terrifying and comforting, and as Mary sat in the darkened room, the storm inside her finally began to quiet.

Chapter 22
The Final Confrontation

The night was heavy with silence, the kind that settled deep into the bones and refused to let go. Mary sat in the children's room, her back pressed against the wall, the stuffed bear clutched tightly in her hands. The soft glow of the nightlight bathed the room in a faint amber hue, but it did nothing to ease the darkness pressing in around her.

Her mind was a whirlpool of emotions—fear, anger, sorrow, and something darker, something she couldn't name but felt in every trembling breath. The whispers had returned, faint and indistinct, like the distant rustle of leaves in the wind.

"They're gone," they said, their voices low and mournful. "You failed them."

Mary shook her head violently, her tears spilling onto her cheeks. "I didn't fail," she whispered, her voice trembling. "I did everything for them. Everything."

"They're not real," the whispers replied, their tone sharp and accusatory.

"You were never enough."

The words cut through her like a blade, and she let out a strangled sob, her chest heaving with the weight of her grief.

She had built her life around Emily and Daniel; around the love and purpose they had given her. Without them, she was nothing. Empty. Lost.

But one thought lingered in her mind, clinging to her like a lifeline. Thomas. He had planted the seed of doubt, shattering the fragile world she had so carefully constructed. He had to answer for that. He had to understand what he had done.

Mary stood abruptly, the bear slipping from her grasp and landing on the floor. Her movements were deliberate as she grabbed her coat and slipped the knife into her pocket. The weight of it was familiar now, a comforting reminder of the control she still had.

The rain had started again, a steady drizzle that soaked through her clothes as she made her way to Thomas's house. The streets were deserted, the faint glow of streetlights reflecting off the wet pavement. Mary's footsteps were muffled by the rain, her breathing steady despite the storm raging inside her.

When she reached his house, the sight of the blue shutters and the warm light spilling from the windows made her chest tighten. She stood there for a moment, her hand trembling as she reached for the doorbell.

Thomas opened the door almost immediately, his expression shifting from surprise to concern when he saw her. "Mary," he said, his tone soft. "What are you doing here? It's late."

Mary stepped inside without waiting for an invitation, her wet shoes squeaking against the hardwood floor. She turned to face him, her hands clenched at her sides.

"We need to talk," she said, her voice trembling but firm.

Thomas hesitated, his gaze flickering to her soaked coat and dishevelled appearance. "Of course," he said gently. "Let me get you a towel."

"No," Mary snapped, her voice sharper than she intended. "This can't wait."

Thomas stopped, his brow furrowing as he studied her. "Okay," he said cautiously. "What's going on?"

Mary took a deep breath, her chest tightening as she searched for the right words. "You destroyed everything," she said finally, her voice breaking. "You made me doubt them."

Thomas's confusion deepened. "Mary, I don't understand—"

"My children," she interrupted, her tears spilling over. "You told me they weren't real. You made me question everything."

Thomas's expression softened; his concern etched deeply into his features. "Mary," he said carefully, "I wasn't trying to hurt you. I just—"

"Stop," Mary said, her voice rising. "Stop pretending like you care. You don't understand what you've done."

Thomas took a step closer, his hands raised in a gesture of peace. "You're right," he said gently. "I don't understand. But I want to. Let me help you."

The sincerity in his voice brought a lump to Mary's throat, but it also fuelled her anger. She couldn't trust him. Not now. Not after everything he had done.

"You can't help me," she said bitterly. "You've already ruined everything."

Mary's hand slipped into her pocket, her fingers closing around the knife. The weight of it was both comforting and terrifying, a stark reminder of the power she still held. Her chest heaved as she pulled it out, the blade glinting in the dim light.

Thomas's eyes widened, his body tensing as he took a step back. "Mary," he said carefully, his voice steady despite the fear in his eyes. "You don't have to do this."

"You don't get to tell me what I have to do," Mary said, her voice trembling with emotion. "You took them from me. You made me question everything I believed in. And now… now there's nothing left."

Thomas remained still, his gaze steady but cautious. "I didn't take anything from you," he said gently. "I want to help you find the truth."

Mary let out a bitter laugh, the sound hollow and broken. "The truth?" she spat. "The truth is that I have nothing. No children. No family. Nothing."

"That's not true," Thomas said, his tone firm but kind. "You're not alone, Mary. I'm here. Let me help you."

Mary's hands shook as she gripped the knife, her vision blurring with tears. She wanted to believe him, to trust the warmth in his voice and the sincerity in his eyes. But the pain and anger were too strong, drowning out any flicker of hope.

"You can't help me," she whispered, her voice breaking. "No one can."

The room seemed to freeze as Mary lunged forward, the knife slashing through the air. Thomas reacted quickly, grabbing her wrist and twisting it, forcing the blade from her hand. It clattered to the floor as they struggled, their movements frantic and desperate.

"Mary, stop!" Thomas shouted, his voice filled with equal parts fear and concern. "You don't have to do this!"

But Mary couldn't hear him. The whispers had returned, louder than ever, their voices blending into a cacophony of fear and desperation.

"Protect them," they said. "Don't let him win."

Thomas managed to pin Mary's arms, his grip firm but careful. "Listen to me," he said urgently. "You're not alone. I'm not your enemy. Please, Mary, let me help you."

Mary froze, her chest heaving as she stared at him, her tears streaming down her face. For a moment, the room was silent except for the sound of their ragged breathing. The warmth in Thomas's eyes cut through the chaos in her mind, and for the first time, she felt the faintest flicker of clarity.

But it was too late.

Mary let out a choked sob as she slumped against Thomas, her body trembling with exhaustion. The knife lay forgotten on the floor, its blade glinting in the dim light. Thomas held her carefully, his voice soft and steady as he murmured words of comfort.

"It's okay," he said. "You're safe now. We'll get through this together."

But Mary didn't feel safe. She felt broken, her world shattered beyond repair. The whispers had gone silent, leaving her alone with the weight of her grief and guilt.

"I'm sorry," she whispered, her voice barely audible. "I'm so sorry."

Thomas held her tighter, his concern etched deeply into his features. "It's not too late," he said softly. "We can fix this. You just have to let me help."

Mary closed her eyes, her tears falling freely as she clung to him. For the first time, she allowed herself to hope that maybe—just maybe—there was a way out of the darkness.

But deep down, she knew the truth.
Some things could never be fixed.

Chapter 23
Fractured Pieces

The room was heavy with silence. The faint hum of Thomas's refrigerator in the adjoining kitchen was the only sound, a quiet reminder that the rest of the world continued turning, oblivious to the storm that had just raged inside his home. Mary sat slumped on the couch, her head in her hands, her body trembling with exhaustion. The knife lay discarded on the floor between her and Thomas, its presence a stark reminder of how far things had spiralled.

Thomas stood a few feet away, his hands still shaking as he ran them through his hair. He hadn't spoken since he'd wrestled the blade from her grip, his mind racing to process what had just happened. The woman sitting before him, the same woman who had seemed fragile yet composed just weeks ago, was now a shattered shell of herself. And yet, as much as he wanted to distance himself, to tell her to leave and never come back, he couldn't. Something about her pain felt familiar, resonating with a part of himself he didn't fully understand.

"Mary," he said finally, his voice soft but firm. "I think we need to talk about what's really going on here."

She didn't respond at first. Her shoulders rose and fell with uneven breaths, and when she finally lifted her head, her tear-streaked face was a mixture of anger and despair.

"What's the point?" she asked bitterly. "You've already decided I'm crazy. Everyone has."

"I haven't decided anything," Thomas replied, keeping his tone steady. "I just want to understand. Help me understand."

Mary's laugh was hollow, her hands tightening into fists. "Understand what? That I've lost everything? That the only thing keeping me going was a lie? How do you even begin to 'understand' that?"

Thomas hesitated, his gaze softening. He wanted to say something comforting, something that would ease the sharp edges of her pain, but the words wouldn't come. Instead, he moved to sit in the chair across from her, his movements slow and deliberate, as though approaching a wounded animal.

"You're not alone in this," he said carefully. "I know it feels like you are, but you're not."

Mary scoffed, shaking her head. "What does that even mean? You don't know what it's like to live every day fighting to hold onto something, only to realise it was never real."

Thomas leaned forward, resting his elbows on his knees. "You're right," he admitted. "I don't know what that's like. But I do know what it's like to feel lost, to feel like nothing you do matters." He paused, his jaw tightening. "I've been there."

Mary's eyes narrowed, suspicion flickering across her face. "What are you talking about?"

Thomas hesitated, his gaze dropping to the floor. "I don't talk about this much," he said quietly. "But a few years ago, I lost someone. Someone I cared about deeply." His voice faltered, the words catching in his throat. "She was my sister. We were close, but I didn't see how much she was struggling. I didn't know how to help her."

Mary frowned, the sharpness in her expression softening. "What happened?"

"She... she took her own life," Thomas said, his voice barely above a whisper. "And I blamed myself. For years, I carried that guilt, convinced that if I'd just done something differently, said something sooner, she'd still be here."

Mary's chest tightened as she listened, her anger fading into something else—something closer to empathy. For the first time, she saw the cracks in Thomas's calm exterior, the pain he kept hidden beneath his steady demeanour.

"I'm sorry," she said softly, the words feeling inadequate but genuine.

Thomas nodded; his gaze distant. "I don't tell you this to make you feel sorry for me," he said. "I just... I want you to know that I understand what it's like to feel like you're drowning. But Mary, you don't have to go through this alone. You can let someone in."

Mary looked away, her hands trembling in her lap. She wanted to believe him, wanted to believe that there was still a way forward. But the weight of her grief and guilt was suffocating, crushing her under its relentless pressure.

"I don't know how to fix this," she admitted, her voice barely audible. "I don't even know where to start."

"You start by letting go of the blame," Thomas said gently. "You've carried this burden for so long, but it's not yours to carry alone."

Mary let out a shaky breath, her tears spilling over again. "It's not that simple."

"I know it's not," Thomas said. "But you've already taken the first step. You're here, talking to me. That's a start."

The room fell silent again, the weight of their shared vulnerability hanging heavy in the air. Mary stared at the floor, her mind racing with thoughts she couldn't articulate. She felt raw, exposed, as though Thomas had peeled back the layers of her carefully constructed defences and laid her bare.

For the first time in years, she felt the faintest flicker of hope.

The moment was broken by the sound of Mary's phone buzzing in her coat pocket. She flinched at the sudden noise, her heart racing as she fumbled to retrieve it. When she saw the number on the screen, her stomach dropped.

"It's the police," she said, her voice shaking.

Thomas's brow furrowed. "Why would they be calling you?"

Mary didn't answer. Her hands trembled as she stared at the phone, her mind racing. The whispers that had been silent returned, faint but insistent.

"They know," they said. "They're coming for you."

"Answer it," Thomas urged gently. "It's better to face whatever this is head-on."

Mary hesitated for a moment before pressing the button to accept the call. Her voice was unsteady as she answered. "Hello?"

"Ms. Stewart?" The voice on the other end was calm but firm. "This is Detective Harris with the local police department. We need to speak with you regarding an ongoing investigation. Are you available to come to the station?"

Mary's blood ran cold. Her throat felt tight, and for a moment, she couldn't speak. "I... I don't understand," she stammered. "What is this about?"

"It would be best if we discussed this in person," Detective Harris said. "Can you come down to the station today?"

Mary's grip on the phone tightened, her chest heaving. "I... I don't know," she said weakly. "I need some time."

"Ms. Stewart, this is important," Harris said, his tone firm but not unkind. "Please let us know when you're ready to come in."

The call ended before Mary could respond, and she let the phone slip from her fingers, her body trembling. She turned to Thomas, her eyes wide with fear.

"They know," she whispered, her voice trembling. "They know everything."

Thomas frowned, his concern deepening. "Mary, what are you talking about? What do they know?"

"The women," Mary said, her voice breaking. "The ones I... the ones I hurt."

Thomas's face paled, his expression shifting from confusion to shock. "Mary," he said carefully. "What are you saying?"

"I didn't mean to," Mary sobbed, her hands flying to her face. "I just... I couldn't stop. The whispers—they told me to do it."

Thomas stared at her, his mind racing as he tried to process her words. "You're telling me you... you killed those women?"

Mary nodded, her body shaking with the force of her sobs. "I didn't want to," she whispered. "But I couldn't help it. I was trying to protect them. Emily and Daniel."

Thomas's chest tightened as he realised the full extent of her delusions. The pieces of the puzzle clicked into place, and he felt a surge of anger, fear, and pity all at once. He wanted to comfort her, to tell her that everything would be okay, but he knew it wouldn't. Not anymore.

"Mary," he said softly, his voice trembling. "We need to go to the police. You need help."

Mary looked up at him, her eyes wide with terror. "No," she said firmly. "I can't. They'll take me away. They'll lock me up."

"They might," Thomas admitted, his voice breaking. "But they can also get you the help you need. This can't go on like this."

Mary shook her head violently, backing away from him. "You don't understand," she said, her voice rising. "I can't lose them. I can't."

Thomas took a step toward her, his hands raised in a gesture of peace. "Mary, please," he said. "Let me help you. We can figure this out together."

But Mary was already retreating, her back hitting the doorframe as her breathing grew rapid and shallow. The whispers were louder now, their voices drowning out everything else.

"You can't trust him," they said. "You have to protect yourself."

Mary turned and bolted out the door, the storm outside engulfing her as Thomas called after her, his voice filled with desperation.

"Mary, wait!"

But she didn't stop. She couldn't. The fractures in her mind had grown.

Mary ran into the storm, her heart pounding in her chest as she fled from Thomas's house. The rain fell harder now, drenching her as her feet pounded against the slick pavement. The whispers screamed in her ears, their voices blending into a cacophony of fear and desperation.

"Run!" they shouted. "You can't let him stop you!"

The streetlights flickered in the downpour, their pale glow distorted by the rain. Mary's vision blurred, her tears mixing with the water streaming down her face. She didn't know where she was going—she only knew she had to get away. Away from Thomas. Away from the truth. Away from the crushing realisation that her entire world had been built on a lie.

The memories came unbidden as she ran, flashing through her mind like shards of broken glass. Emily's laughter as she played with her stuffed bear. Daniel's shy smile as he proudly showed her the drawing he'd made. Their voices, their warmth, their love—it had felt so real. But now those memories were unravelling, slipping through her grasp like smoke.

"They're not gone," the whispers insisted. "They're still here. You just have to protect them."

Mary stumbled, her knees scraping against the wet pavement as she fell. She let out a cry of pain, clutching her hands against the ground as the rain continued to fall around her. For a moment, she stayed there, her body trembling as she gasped for air.

"They're still here," she whispered, her voice trembling. "They have to be."

But no matter how many times she repeated the words, they felt hollow. The doubt that had been gnawing at her for weeks was now an unrelenting weight in her chest, threatening to crush her.

When she finally forced herself to stand, her legs felt weak, unsteady beneath her. She looked around, her surroundings unfamiliar in the darkness and rain. The streets were deserted, the houses dark and silent. She didn't recognise where she was, and for the first time, fear crept into her chest.

Her phone buzzed in her pocket, the vibration startling her. She pulled it out with trembling hands, the screen glowing faintly in the darkness. It was a message from Thomas.

Thomas: Mary, please come back. We can figure this out together. You don't have to do this alone.

Her fingers hovered over the screen, her breath hitching in her throat. She wanted to believe him, to trust the sincerity in his words. But the whispers returned, their voices sharp and insistent.

"He's lying," they said. "He wants to take you away. He wants to destroy everything."

Mary clenched her teeth, her hands trembling as she shoved the phone back into her pocket. She couldn't trust him. Not now. Not after everything.

She kept walking, her footsteps unsteady as the rain soaked through her clothes. Her mind raced, the whispers filling her thoughts with images of betrayal and loss. She thought of the women she had killed, their faces a blur in her memory. She thought of Thomas, his calm, measured words cutting through her like a blade.

And she thought of Emily and Daniel, their absence leaving an ache in her chest that felt unbearable.

The whispers grew louder, their tone shifting from anger to urgency. "You need to go back," they said. "You need to make things right."

Mary stopped in her tracks, her breath coming in short, ragged gasps. "Make things right?" she whispered, her voice trembling. "How?"

The whispers didn't answer. Instead, they filled her mind with images—of her children, of the women she had killed, of Thomas's face as he pleaded with her to stop. The images blended together, a chaotic swirl of memories and delusions that left her feeling dizzy and disoriented.

"I can't," she whispered, her tears falling freely. "I can't fix this."

By the time Mary returned to her house, the storm had begun to wane, the rain now a faint drizzle. She stood on the front steps, her body trembling as she stared at the door. The house looked different now—empty, lifeless, a hollow shell of the home she had imagined for herself and her children.

She stepped inside, the silence pressing down on her like a weight. The air was cold, heavy with the scent of rain and damp wood. She made her way up the stairs, her footsteps slow and deliberate, each one feeling heavier than the last.

When she reached the children's room, she hesitated, her hand resting on the doorknob. Her chest tightened as she pushed the door open, her breath catching in her throat.

The room was exactly as she had left it—perfectly tidy, untouched. Emily's pink quilt was smooth and pristine, the stuffed bear sitting upright on her pillow. Daniel's blue comforter was neatly tucked, the books on the shelves perfectly aligned.

Mary stepped inside, her hands trembling as she picked up the bear. She clutched it to her chest, her tears soaking into the worn fabric.

"I'm sorry," she whispered, her voice breaking. "I tried so hard. I just… I didn't know."

The room remained silent; its stillness oppressive. Mary sank to the floor, her body trembling as the weight of her grief and guilt consumed her.

The sound of the front door opening startled her, and she froze, her breath hitching in her throat. She heard footsteps, slow and cautious, making their way up the stairs.

"Mary?" Thomas's voice called softly. "Are you here?"

Her chest tightened as she clutched the bear tighter, her mind racing. The whispers returned; their voices urgent.

"You can't let him win," they said. "You have to protect yourself."

"Mary," Thomas said again, his voice closer now. "Please, talk to me. Let me help you."

The door to the children's room creaked open, and Thomas stepped inside, his gaze soft but determined. He took in the sight of her—curled on the floor, clutching the stuffed bear—and his expression softened.

"Mary," he said gently. "It's going to be okay. I promise."

But Mary shook her head, her tears streaming down her face. "You don't understand," she said, her voice trembling. "I've lost everything."

"You haven't," Thomas said firmly. "You can still find a way forward. But you have to let me help you."

Mary's hands trembled as she looked up at him, her eyes filled with fear and desperation. "I don't know how," she whispered. "I don't know how to fix this."

Thomas took a step closer, his movements slow and deliberate. "You start by trusting someone," he said. "Let me help you, Mary. Please."

For a moment, Mary felt the faintest flicker of hope. But the whispers returned, their voices louder than ever.

"He'll destroy you," they said. "He'll take everything."

Mary let out a choked sob, her body trembling as the storm inside her mind raged on. She didn't know what was real anymore, didn't know who to trust. All she knew was the pain and the fear, the unrelenting weight of her broken reality.

And in that moment, she made a decision.

Chapter 24
The Breaking of the Veil

The air in the children's room felt heavier than ever, suffocating in its stillness. Mary remained seated on the floor, her knees drawn to her chest, clutching Emily's bear so tightly that her fingers ached. The faint hum of the nightlight cast long shadows across the walls, creating the illusion of movement where there was none.

Thomas stood a few feet away, his hands at his sides, his expression filled with a mix of concern and heartbreak. He didn't move closer; he didn't need to. The tension between them was a living thing, stretching taut and fragile like a thread about to snap.

"Mary," he said softly, his voice breaking the silence. "You don't have to live like this anymore."

She didn't look at him. Her eyes remained fixed on the bear, her tears soaking into its fur. "You don't understand," she whispered, her voice trembling. "They're all I have. Without them, I'm nothing."

Thomas took a cautious step closer, his movements deliberate, his tone gentle. "Mary, I know it feels that way. But they're not real. You've been carrying this pain for so long, and it's—"

"Stop it!" Mary snapped, her voice sharp and brittle. She looked up at him, her face streaked with tears. "You don't get to tell me what's real and what isn't. You don't know what I've been through!"

Thomas froze, his hands raised in a gesture of peace. "You're right," he said carefully. "I don't know what you've been through. But I can see how much you're hurting. And I just... I want to help."

Mary let out a bitter laugh, the sound hollow and broken. "Help?" she said, shaking her head. "No one can help me. Not anymore."

The whispers returned, faint at first, their tone urgent.

"He's lying," they said.

"He'll take everything from you."

Mary's breathing quickened, her chest heaving as the voices grew louder. She clenched her fists, her nails digging into her palms. "I don't know what to believe anymore," she whispered, her voice breaking.

"Believe what you feel," the whispers urged. "Protect what's yours."

Her gaze shifted to Thomas, who was still watching her with a mixture of caution and concern. His presence felt overwhelming, his calm, steady demeanour a stark contrast to the chaos inside her mind. She hated him for it—for the way he made her question everything, for the way he had broken the fragile world she had built for herself.

"Why are you doing this?" she demanded, her voice trembling. "Why can't you just leave me alone?"

Thomas hesitated, his brow furrowing as he searched for the right words. "Because I care about you, Mary," he said finally. "I see so much of myself in you—so much pain, so much loss. And I don't want you to go through this alone."

The sincerity in his voice cut through her anger, leaving her feeling raw and exposed. For a moment, the whispers quieted, their voices fading into the background. But the silence didn't bring her peace. Instead, it left her with the crushing weight of her grief and guilt.

I don't deserve your help," Mary said, her voice barely above a whisper. "I don't deserve anything."

"That's not true," Thomas said firmly. He took another step closer, his movements slow and deliberate. "You deserve to heal. You deserve a chance to move forward."

Mary shook her head, her tears falling freely. "I can't," she said. "It's too late."

"It's never too late," Thomas said, his voice steady. "But you have to let me in. You have to trust me."

Mary looked up at him, her eyes filled with fear and desperation. "How can I trust you when I can't even trust myself?" she asked, her voice breaking.

Thomas didn't have an answer. Instead, he knelt down in front of her, his movements careful and deliberate. He reached out, his hand hovering just above hers. "You're stronger than you think," he said softly. "And you don't have to do this alone."

For a moment, Mary allowed herself to believe him. She allowed herself to imagine a world where she didn't have to carry the weight of her pain alone, where she could let someone else share her burden. But the whispers returned, their voices sharp and insistent.

"He'll destroy you," they said. "You can't let him win."

Mary's body tensed, her chest tightening as the storm inside her mind raged on. She clutched the bear tighter, her knuckles white as she fought to quiet the voices. But they wouldn't be silenced. They demanded action.

"Protect yourself," they urged. "Protect your children."

Her gaze flickered to the knife on the floor, its blade glinting faintly in the dim light. She hadn't even realised Thomas had set it there, far from her reach, but close enough to remind her of its presence. The sight of it made her stomach churn, a mix of fear and resolve taking hold.

Thomas noticed her gaze and followed it to the knife. His expression shifted, his eyes widening slightly as he realised what she was thinking. "Mary," he said carefully, his voice calm but firm. "Don't do this. You don't have to fight anymore. You don't have to protect them—they're gone."

The words hit her like a blow, knocking the air from her lungs. Her grip on the bear loosened, and it slipped from her hands, landing on the floor with a soft thud. "They're not gone," she said, her voice trembling. "They're still here. I can feel them."

"They're not," Thomas said gently, his tone filled with sorrow. "And that's not your fault. But holding on to them this way—it's only hurting you."

Mary shook her head, her tears streaming down her face. "You don't understand," she whispered. "They're all I have. Without them, I'm nothing."

"You're not nothing," Thomas said firmly. "You're still here. You still have a chance to find peace. But you have to let go."

The words echoed in her mind, cutting through the chaos like a blade. She wanted to believe him, wanted to let go of the pain and the guilt that had consumed her for so long. But the thought of letting go felt impossible, like severing a part of herself she couldn't live without.

"I don't know how," she admitted, her voice breaking.

"You don't have to do it all at once," Thomas said. "You just have to take the first step."

Mary looked at him, her vision blurred by tears. For a moment, she saw something in his eyes that she hadn't seen in a long time—hope. It was faint and fragile, but it was there. And for the first time, she allowed herself to reach for it.

But the whispers wouldn't let her go so easily.

"He's lying," they said, their voices sharp and urgent. "He doesn't care about you. He wants to destroy everything."

Mary's chest tightened, her breathing growing rapid as the voices grew louder. She pressed her hands to her ears, shaking her head violently. "Stop," she whispered. "Please, stop."

Thomas reached for her, his hand resting gently on her shoulder. "Mary," he said softly. "You're stronger than this. Don't let them control you."

His touch was grounding, a lifeline in the storm. But it wasn't enough. The whispers were too loud, their voices too strong. Mary's gaze flickered to the knife again, and in that moment, something inside her snapped.

She lunged for the blade, her fingers closing around the handle as she turned toward Thomas. His eyes widened in shock, and he grabbed her wrists, his grip firm but careful.

"Mary, stop!" he shouted, his voice filled with desperation.

But she couldn't hear him. The whispers had taken over, their voices drowning out everything else. She struggled against him, her body trembling with the force of her emotions.

"I have to protect them," she sobbed. "I have to."

"They're gone!" Thomas shouted, his voice breaking. "There's no one left to protect!"

The words hit her like a tidal wave, and she froze, her chest heaving as the knife slipped from her grasp. It clattered to the floor, and Thomas pulled her into his arms, holding her tightly as she sobbed uncontrollably.

"I'm so sorry," she whispered, her voice barely audible. "I'm so sorry."

Thomas held her close, his own tears falling as he whispered softly, "It's not your fault. You're not alone anymore. You're not alone."

Chapter 25
The Veil Falls

The house was still. The faint hum of the refrigerator in the kitchen seemed deafening in the silence that followed Mary's collapse into Thomas's arms. The storm outside had quieted, leaving the world damp and heavy, the rain-soaked air filtering in through the cracked window in the children's room. It carried the faint scent of wet earth and something sharper, a reminder of the battle that had just played out within these walls.

Mary's sobs had subsided into quiet, hiccupping breaths, her body trembling in Thomas's arms. He held her tightly, his grip firm but gentle, as though afraid that letting go would send her spiralling back into the darkness she had been fighting to escape.

"You're safe now," he murmured, his voice low and steady. "You don't have to do this alone anymore."

But Mary shook her head, her face buried in his chest. "I don't know how to let go," she whispered, her voice barely audible. "They were my everything. Without them, I'm nothing."

Thomas closed his eyes, his heart aching at the raw pain in her words. He wanted to tell her she was wrong, that she was so much more than her delusions, but he knew words wouldn't be enough. Not now. Not after everything.

"You're not nothing," he said finally, his voice firm. "You're still here, Mary. You still have a chance to heal."

Mary pulled back slightly, her tear-streaked face etched with doubt. "How?" she asked, her voice trembling. "How do I heal from this? From losing everything?"

Thomas hesitated, searching for the right words. "It's not going to be easy," he admitted. "It's going to take time. But the first step is letting someone in. Let me help you."

For a moment, Mary seemed to consider his words. Her gaze flickered to the stuffed bear lying on the floor, its button eyes glinting faintly in the dim light. The sight of it brought fresh tears to her eyes, and she turned away, unable to face the reminder of the life she had built and lost.

"I don't think I can do this," she said softly, her voice breaking. "It hurts too much."

Thomas reached out, placing a hand gently on her shoulder. "I know it hurts," he said. "But you're stronger than you think. You've been carrying this pain for so long, and you're still here. That says something."

Mary let out a bitter laugh, shaking her head. "I'm not strong," she said. "I'm broken. I've done terrible things, Thomas. Things I can't take back."

Thomas's chest tightened, the weight of her confession pressing down on him. He thought of the women who had been murdered, the brutality of the crimes, and the fear that had gripped the community. And yet, as he looked at Mary now, trembling and tearful, he couldn't bring himself to hate her. All he saw was a woman drowning in her own pain, desperate for a way out.

I can't undo what I've done," Mary said, her voice trembling. "And I can't live with it, either. I don't know how to move forward."

"You don't have to figure it all out right now," Thomas said gently. "One step at a time. That's all you need to focus on."

Mary looked at him, her eyes filled with desperation. "You make it sound so simple," she said. "But it's not. It's never been simple."

"I know it's not," Thomas said. "But you've already taken the first step by admitting the truth. That takes strength, Mary. More strength than you realise."

The room fell silent again, the weight of their conversation hanging heavy in the air. Mary stared at the floor, her hands trembling in her lap. She wanted to believe Thomas, to trust that there was a way forward. But the darkness inside her felt insurmountable, a chasm too deep to cross.

Thomas stood and moved to the door, his movements slow and deliberate. "I'll give you some space," he said. "But I'll be just downstairs if you need me."

Mary didn't respond, her gaze fixed on the floor. Thomas hesitated for a moment, his concern etched into his features, before stepping out of the room and closing the door behind him.

The silence that followed was deafening. Mary sat motionless for a long time, her mind a chaotic swirl of emotions. The whispers had gone quiet, leaving her alone with her thoughts. She stared at the stuffed bear on the floor, her chest tightening with a mix of grief and guilt.

When she finally moved, it was with a sense of purpose that felt foreign after so many weeks of chaos. She picked up the bear, smoothing its fur with trembling hands before setting it gently on Emily's bed. She straightened the pink quilt, her movements careful and deliberate, as though the act of tidying the room could somehow restore what had been lost.

But no matter how much she tried to create order, the emptiness remained. The room was perfect, untouched, a shrine to a life that had never existed. And as Mary stood there, the weight of that realisation pressed down on her, suffocating in its intensity.

Downstairs, Thomas paced the living room, his mind racing. He felt a deep sense of unease, an instinctive awareness that something wasn't right. He had seen the look in Mary's eyes before he left the room—the despair, the hopelessness. It gnawed at him, urging him to go back, to make sure she was okay.

But he hesitated. He didn't want to push her, didn't want to risk shattering the fragile progress they had made. He told himself to give her time, to let her process everything on her own.

A sudden noise from upstairs broke his train of thought—a muffled thud that sent a jolt of fear through his chest. He didn't wait. He bolted up the stairs, his heart pounding as he reached the children's room.

The sight that greeted him stopped him in his tracks. Mary was on the floor, her body slumped against the bed. Her face was pale, her eyes closed, and a small bottle of pills lay on its side beside her.

"Mary!" Thomas shouted, rushing to her side. He dropped to his knees, his hands trembling as he shook her gently. "Mary, wake up!"

She didn't respond. Her breathing was shallow, her pulse faint beneath his fingertips. Panic surged through Thomas as he reached for his phone, dialling 911 with shaking hands.

The minutes that followed felt like an eternity. Thomas stayed by Mary's side, his voice shaking as he pleaded with her to hold on.

"Don't do this," he whispered, his tears falling freely. "You're stronger than this. You can fight this."

When the paramedics arrived, Thomas stepped back, his hands trembling as they worked to stabilise her. He watched as they lifted her onto a stretcher, his chest tight with a mix of fear and helplessness.

As they wheeled her out of the house, one of the paramedics turned to Thomas. "Are you family?" she asked.

Thomas hesitated, his mind racing. "I'm... a friend," he said finally. "Please, let me know how she's doing."

The paramedic nodded, her expression sympathetic. "We'll do everything we can."

Thomas stood on the porch as the ambulance disappeared into the night, the weight of everything that had happened pressing down on him like a physical force. He felt hollow, his mind a whirlwind of emotions. He had tried to save her, to help her, but it hadn't been enough.

As he turned to go back inside, his gaze fell on the children's room. The door was ajar, the faint glow of the nightlight spilling into the hallway. He stepped inside, his chest tightening as he took in the sight of the perfectly arranged beds, the neatly aligned books, the stuffed bear sitting upright on the pillow.

It was a shrine to a life that had never existed. A haunting reminder of the woman he had tried to save.

Thomas sank to the floor, his head in his hands as the weight of it all came crashing down. The world felt darker now, heavier, as though the hope he had tried so desperately to hold onto had been extinguished.

And in that moment, something inside him shifted. The compassion that had driven him to help Mary was still there, but it was tempered by something darker—an anger, a sense of injustice that burnt deep within him.

He thought of the women Mary had killed, the lives she had destroyed in her quest to protect her children. He thought of the pain she had caused, the chaos she had left in her wake. And he thought of the system that had failed her, the cracks that had allowed her to fall through unnoticed.

As Thomas sat in the silent room, a cold determination took hold. He had tried to save Mary, but he had failed. And now, as he stared at the empty beds and the worn stuffed bear, he made a vow.

He wouldn't fail again.

Epilogue
The Beginning of the End

The hospital room was quiet, save for the faint beeping of the machines that monitored Mary's vital signs. The sterile scent of disinfectant hung in the air, sharp and unforgiving. Thomas sat in a chair near the bed, his elbows resting on his knees, his hands clasped tightly together. He hadn't slept since the ambulance had taken Mary away, and the weight of exhaustion pressed down on him like a physical force.

Mary lay motionless in the bed, her face pale and drawn. The IV in her arm dripped steadily, delivering the fluids and medication that were keeping her alive. Her chest rose and fell in shallow breaths, her body a fragile shell of the woman she had once been.

Thomas stared at her, his mind a whirlwind of emotions. He felt anger, sorrow, guilt, and something darker that he couldn't quite name. He had tried to help her, to pull her back from the edge, but it hadn't been enough. The realisation left a bitter taste in his mouth.

The doctor had spoken to him earlier, explaining Mary's condition in calm, clinical terms. She had survived the overdose, but just barely. The damage to her body and mind was severe, and her recovery—if it happened at all—would be long and uncertain.

"She'll need intensive therapy," the doctor had said, his tone neutral but firm. "And a secure facility where she can get the help she needs. This isn't something she can recover from on her own."

Thomas had nodded, his throat tight with emotion. He knew the doctor was right, but the thought of Mary being locked away in a sterile, impersonal institution felt wrong. She had spent so long trapped in her own mind, isolated and afraid. He didn't want her to feel abandoned again.

The nurses came and went, checking Mary's vitals, adjusting the machines, and leaving without a word. Thomas barely noticed them. His focus remained on Mary, his mind replaying the events of the past few weeks in an endless loop. He thought of the first time they had met, her nervous smile and quiet demeanour. He thought of the moments when she had let her guard down, revealing glimpses of the pain she carried. And he thought of the moment she had lunged for the knife, her face a mask of fear and desperation.

He had seen her at her lowest, her most vulnerable, and he couldn't shake the feeling that he had failed her. He had tried to save her, to help her see that she wasn't alone, but it hadn't been enough. The weight of that failure pressed down on him, leaving him hollow and numb.

As the hours passed, the sky outside the hospital window shifted from grey to black, the city lights casting a faint glow over the room. Thomas hadn't moved from his seat, his gaze fixed on Mary's face. He thought of the women she had killed, the lives she had taken in her quest to protect her imagined children. He thought of the fear and pain she had caused, the ripples of grief that had spread through the community.

And yet, as he looked at her now, he couldn't hate her. He couldn't see her as a monster or a killer. All he saw was a woman who had been consumed by her pain, a woman who had lost herself in the depths of her own mind.

He let out a shaky breath, his hands tightening into fists. The world was cruel and unforgiving, a place where people like Mary were left to fend for themselves until it was too late. The system had failed her, and in doing so, it had failed everyone she had hurt. The thought made his chest ache with a mix of anger and sorrow.

In the days that followed, Thomas found himself visiting Mary's hospital room regularly. He brought books, though he rarely read them, and sat by her bedside for hours at a time. The nurses began to recognise him, offering small smiles and polite nods as they went about their work. He didn't speak much, but his presence was constant, a quiet reassurance in the sterile, impersonal environment.

Mary remained unresponsive, her body still and her mind locked away. Thomas wondered what she was thinking, if she was reliving the moments that had brought her here or if she had found some semblance of peace in the darkness. The uncertainty gnawed at him, leaving him restless and unsettled.

One afternoon, as he sat by her bed, a nurse approached with a clipboard in hand. "Mr. Greene?" she asked, her voice soft but professional.

Thomas looked up, his expression weary. "Yes?"

"We need to discuss Mary's care plan moving forward," the nurse said. "The doctors are recommending that she be transferred to a long-term psychiatric facility. It's the best option for her recovery."

Thomas nodded slowly, the words sinking in like stones. He had known this moment was coming, but it still felt like a blow. "Where would she go?" he asked, his voice low.

The nurse hesitated, her gaze sympathetic. "There's a facility nearby," she said. "It's secure, with a focus on intensive therapy and rehabilitation. It's not perfect, but it's the best place for her right now."

Thomas let out a heavy sigh, his shoulders slumping. "Can I visit her there?"

The nurse offered a small smile. "Of course," she said. "She'll need all the support she can get."

That night, Thomas returned home, the emptiness of his apartment pressing down on him. He sat in the dark for hours, his mind racing with thoughts he couldn't quiet. He thought of Mary, lying motionless in her hospital bed, and of the life she had imagined for herself. He thought of the women she had killed, their lives cut short by her pain and delusion.

And he thought of the system that had failed her, the cracks that had allowed her to fall through unnoticed. The injustice of it all burned in his chest, a slow, simmering anger that refused to be ignored.

He had tried to help her, to save her, but it hadn't been enough. And now, as he sat alone in the silence, he felt a dark resolve taking hold. He couldn't undo what had been done, but he could make sure it didn't happen again. He could make sure the world didn't forget Mary, or the women she had hurt, or the pain that had driven her to the edge.

In the weeks that followed, Thomas's visits to Mary became less frequent. He told himself it was because he needed time to process everything, but deep down, he knew the truth. He couldn't bear to see her like that, trapped in a place where he couldn't reach her.

Instead, he threw himself into his work, his days consumed by the routines of the operating theatre. But the darkness inside him remained, a constant presence that whispered in the quiet moments, urging him toward something he couldn't yet define.

He began to see the world differently, the cracks and flaws more pronounced than ever. He saw the pain and suffering that went unnoticed, the people who slipped through the cracks, forgotten and ignored. And he felt the anger growing stronger, feeding the part of him that wanted to take control, to fix what was broken.

One evening, as he sat in his apartment, Thomas pulled out the stuffed bear he had taken from Mary's house. He held it in his hands, the worn fabric soft beneath his fingers. It was a reminder of everything she had lost, everything she had fought to protect. And as he stared at it, he felt the weight of his own loss settle over him.

He hadn't just lost Mary. He had lost a part of himself—the part that believed in the goodness of the world, the part that thought compassion and understanding were enough to make a difference.

The anger that had been simmering inside him finally boiled over, consuming him in its intensity. He clenched the bear tightly, his jaw set as a dark determination took hold.

If the world wouldn't protect the people who needed it most, then he would. And if that meant breaking the rules, stepping outside the lines, then so be it.

As Thomas sat alone in the dark, the first seeds of his transformation were sown. The man he had been was gone, and in his place was someone new. Someone who wouldn't hesitate to do what needed to be done.

Someone who would make the world pay for its failures.